MURDER ON DEATH ISLAND

VAUGHN VALOIS

PROLOGUE

A GENTLE BREEZE carried the smell of the ocean and just a hint of winter chill. The moon was nearly full and her glow added a silver lining to the silhouettes of trees and gave an ethereal glow to the old tarmac road winding its way up the mountains. The sound of birds and the symphony of cicadas quelled as the roar of an engine grew louder. Soon, headlights pierced the night. There was a squeal of rubber as the old Mustang fish-tailed wildly around the hairpin turns. Peals of laughter and surf rock climbed up over the sounds of the motor.

"Whoo!" said Rhonda. "Say, Duke, you sure know how to handle this heap?" The top was down, and her auburn hair was a halo of brown flames leaping about her head.

Though Duke's muscles strained beneath his t-shirt and his veins bulged in his temple, his face was relaxed and easy. Teeth as white as polished pearls glinted as he smiled. He shifted gears, revving the engine. Like a bandit making off with all the gold in Fort Knox, he thought to himself. "Baby, you ain't seen nothing yet!" he called over to her. "Get an eyeful of this!"

The road was climbing higher and higher. The glittering city lights shimmered below like constellations in the inky blackness. A sign announcing a scenic overlook whooshed by. Yellow warning signs screamed about the dangers of falling rocks and sharp turns. They suggested a speed limit that might have been 25 miles per hour, but flashed by too fast to read.

Up around the next turn, the narrow road steepened and appeared to turn into a ramp leading straight up into the cloudless sky.

"DUKE!" Rhonda screamed. "Duke LOOK OUT!!!" The tachometer swung right and left as Duke punched it into high gear, slamming him and Rhonda back into their slick leather seats like astronauts making for the moon. The car was slurping up asphalt like linguine and the ledge to oblivion was coming up fast. Rhonda clutched the door handle until her bloodless knuckles went white. She flung the other arm across her eyes to blot out the sight of certain death.

With a quick heel-toe, Duke downshifted, mashed the brakes, and swung the wheel right for all he was worth. Great clouds of smoke billowed behind them. The smell of burnt rubber and exhaust stung their nostrils. Rhonda's stomach dropped when one of the tires kissed the cliff's edge before climbing back up on solid ground. The road continued up past an unseen bend.

Her screams broke into mad peels of laughter. "Oh, Duke! You're nuts, you know that?! Absolutely nuts!" She leaned over to kiss his cheek. "And you sure do know how to warm up a motor," she said into his ear close enough he could feel her lips graze across them.

"It's easy," Duke said back. "It's all about having the right touch- knowing when to drop the hammer and when to ease up."

"Mmm, I don't think I ever want you to ease up."

Duke looked over to her. Rhonda's soft features looked so right in the pale moonlight. Her full lips, her wild curls billowing everywhere. He leaned over to plant a kiss on her cheek.

"Watch out!" she shouted, raising a finger towards the road ahead. Duke was braking and swerving out of reflex before his eyes could make sense of the road ahead.

"What is it?" he asked.

"I... I don't know. Some kind of animal, I guess." Her brow furrowed briefly, then she shook her head. "Anyhow, is this place coming up soon or what?"

"Sure," said Duke. "In fact, we're practically there." Sure enough, a dirt drive veered off from the paved road around the next bend, forming a sort of crooked "Y." Duke eased up on the gas and took the turnoff. The dirt road cut through a thick swath of trees before opening up to a small overlook. Beyond a low guardrail, the whole island was laid out like an oil painting. Pure serenity. The tires crunched to a halt, and the purring motor cut out. Now there was just stillness, silence, and sweet salty air.

"Mmm," Rhonda hummed. She closed her eyes, breathing in the moment as her heartbeat calmed. Then she laughed sweetly. "Wow, Duke, you were right about this place."

"I'm right about a lot of things," Duke smiled. He stretched his arm around her shoulders. "And the best part is, it looks like we've got the whole place to ourselves." He crushed his lips into hers in a passionate kiss. She melted into his arms and kissed back, all tongue and shudders of warmth rising up from every part of her body. Her slender fingers cradled his taught, muscular neck. Her fingernails scratched down his back. His calloused hands grazed her belly and climbed their way up beneath her blouse, reaching the soft, yielding flesh of her breasts. Her nipples hardened. She reached down his pants and found him hard and stiff. Sometime in the mad frenzy of hands and tongue, arms and legs, they found themselves in the backseat. Duke slid her skirt up high and pulled her panties to one side. Waves of pleasure crashed over her body like breakers across a ship on a stormy sea. His fingers found her and she writhed beneath his touch. Her breath caught in her throat as he slid into her. She moaned. Again and again they kissed and writhed, as one panting beast wild with lust. Together, their passions melted. Rose. Crested. Exploded into a thunderclap of ecstasy. And rolled gently back.

Rhonda stretched out upon the back seat and caught

her breath, looking up into an endless pool of twinkling stars. Duke shook two cigarettes from the case. He lit them both and offered Rhonda one.

"My God! And I thought there was nothing to do on this old rock." Rhonda exhaled the words with her smoke. Her eyes met Duke's. She could see her own moonlit reflection over the deep dark of his eyes. Her hand cradled his cheek. "I love you, Duke."

"I love you too, Rhonda," Duke said, planting a soft kiss on her soft, wet lips. It tasted like ash and paradise.

"Duke, can I ask you something?" They were dressed now and finishing the last few drags of their cigarettes, sitting on the hood of the car.

Duke had his arm around Rhonda's slender shoulder. She rested her head against him and placed her hand on his leg. The hood was warm beneath her, and the breeze felt cool against the sweat of her scalp.

"Fire away," he smiled.

"Do you see a future with us?" she asked. "I mean, after this summer and all?"

"What are you talking about?" Duke said. "Of course I do." He turned to her and lifted her chin with his finger. He saw the moonlight sparkle in the tear that ran down her cheek. "Listen, Rhonda, I talked to my uncle about pulling more hours at the surf shop. The season's coming up, and he'll need extra hands pretty soon. When I save up enough dough, we're taking the first boat off this nothing little rock. So all you need to worry about is where you want to go." He leaned in and gave her ear a playful bite. She laughed.

"I guess... I guess California sounds nice."

"California, huh?" Duke said. He kissed her neck. "Where about?"

"I don't know. LA?"

"I don't know. Sounds pretty dangerous. You're liable to get picked up by some big movie producer. He'll whisk you away to fame and stardom, then I'll never see you again."

"You dummy!" she laughed. "That's half the plan. Only you're coming with me. See, I'll play the queen of the Amazons and you'll be one of the villain's evil henchmen."

"Oh, will I? Mmm. I don't know about that. But I do know I've gotta piss like a racehorse." He slid off the hood of the car. "Don't run off signing any contracts while I'm gone."

Duke headed into the woods. He waded through the underbrush until he found a suitable bush. A feeling of relief washed over him as he unzipped and unleashed a stream all over the dripping leaves of the bush. As the sound of his urine ceased, another sound from behind startled him. It was darker under the cover of the trees. Duke strained his eyes, but it was hard to make out anything but the swaying of the branches in the breeze.

Behind him, a branch snapped. Duke pulled out his switchblade and backed slowly towards the clearing where the Mustang was parked.

"Duke!" Rhonda called. "Duke, what's wrong? Did a tree offer you a bit part in some cut-rate production?"

"Shh! I thought I heard something."

Rhonda listened. Sure enough, there was a sound coming from somewhere in the woods. A strange sound- like a group of people. A rainfall of footsteps. It was getting louder and louder. Approaching at an alarming rate. As if heading straight towards them. "Duke, come on. Let's get out of here!"

Duke's eyes were wide as saucers. He was already running back to the Mustang when something burst forth through the tree line and out into the clearing. It was something so bizarre, Rhonda's mind couldn't register what it was. It was a tangle of legs and arms. A hulking mass descending upon Duke. It brought a fist like a boulder down on Duke's back with a terrible cracking sound.

Rhonda screamed.

Duke struggled onto his hands and knees.

In this wild, frenzied moment, Rhonda thought the abomination now menacing her love bore a striking resemblance to something she had seen before, but her mind was awash in panic and primal fear. She scrambled into the driver's seat. The keys were still in the ignition. She cranked the motor just as Duke dodged another blow from the creature's terrible fist.

He grabbed his switchblade from off the ground and thrust it into the creature with all his might, but it glanced off its hide like a raindrop off a window pane.

Rhonda fumbled frantically to get the car into gear, but had never driven a stick shift. The car stalled with a loud thud. "DUKE!" she screamed.

The creature opened its hand- no!- its claw. Duke ran

with all his might. The beast thrust out its claw and snapped them shut with Duke inside. Blood splattered everywhere. Drops of it fell like a soft rain over Rhonda and the car. When the creature released its grasp, Duke fell apart like a shredded rag doll. His lifeless body, nearly severed in half, collapsed in a pool of blood.

Now a second creature emerged from the clearing.

This time, Rhonda didn't scream. Could not scream. Reality seemed to fall out. All sound fell away. It was as though she were deep underwater. All reality was seen through a soap opera camera with unreal fluidity to its motion. It was as though it wasn't happening to Rhonda, but someone else. The creature swung itself over Duke's mangled remains and lunged towards the car.

It felt as though a stranger was operating her hands and limbs when she turned the key and managed to get the Mustang into reverse, peel backward down the drive, and gun it towards the main road. In a mad moment, the vehicle spun out on the hairpin turn. For a moment, time froze.

Reality came screaming back when the car crunched against the steep mountain wall and the airbag slammed against her face.

Things were in and out from there. She was in the car. She was out of the car. Terrible pain. All pain. Something coming. A rock in her fist. Being lifted high into the air. Trashing. Beating with rock. Slipping. All dark.

PART ONE
ACT I

CHAPTER 1
TOM

THE MOTEL ROOM WAS DARK. A harsh ray of fluorescent street lamp light from outside leaked into the room behind the blackout curtains that were a bit too short to cover the room's single window. Barely illuminated by this, a few empty beer cans and crumpled clothes lay where they had fallen. A laptop lay open but dormant on a small press-board table. In the middle of the room, there was a crummy queen bed. Beneath the stained and crumpled sheets, a man lay naked and sprawled as though he'd fallen off a horse- snoring softly.

More light stabbed through the darkness as the cell phone on the nightstand screamed to life. It rang twice and vibrated halfway off the table before the man reached over and squinted into the face of it.

"NEWS!" read the caller ID. The time read three-thirty-three AM.

The man took a sharp inhale and pressed the green

button. "Yeah?" The voice on the other end of the line spoke for a moment. The man knit his brow. "Christ! Where?" He sat bolt upright. "No, no. I'll be right there." He hung up the call, snapped on the table lamp, and grabbed a shirt and pants from off the floor. He quickly dressed. He stuffed the laptop in his bag. Leaving the light on, he exited the room.

Outside, he was on a second-story landing of stained concrete. Rows of cheap hollow-core doors lead to dozens of identical rooms. The man descended the stairs two at a time. He was jogging across the parking lot when a gruff voice from behind called to him.

"Hey, Walter Cronkite! What's the big story? Is the volcano finally gonna blow?" It came from a gruff man in his late 50s, wearing a dirty tank top.

"Buy an issue today, Jim. It'll be on the cover," said the reporter. He leapt into a sun-weathered Plymouth Valiant. He cranked it a few times before it came to life. Then he gunned it and left the parking lot with tires screeching.

He flew through a couple of yellow lights and one red on the way to his destination. His phone rang again. This time, he answered without checking the caller ID. "This is Tom... Gladys, I-... Yes, he just told me... I'm already on my way... Tell him I'll have the initial report for the website in half an hour... yes... okay bye."

Tom made his way from the cheap district through midtown and turned off to climb up the winding road leading up into the mountains. He followed the road until his way was blocked by a short row of cars and a pair of parked eighteen-wheeler trucks. He abandoned his car in the middle of the road and walked the rest of the way.

The scene ahead flashed red and blue in the light of three police cars. The street was already cordoned off with yellow tape. A tall uniformed officer raised a hand to stop Tom as he approached. Tom flashed a press pass and crouched under the tape.

"No photos," the officer said.

Just ahead, a cherry red Mustang was smashed against the mountainside, trunk first. The driver's side door was open. Inside the cab, airbags hung limp like deflated party balloons. Outside, a pool of blood on the asphalt was labeled with a small yellow marker with a big black number on both sides. Another marker sat in a strange, dark liquid. It must have been a hell of a rear-end collision, Tom thought.

"Was the other car removed?" Tom asked the tall officer.

"Was no other car," said the tall officer.

Tom frowned at the crunched metal, then the pool of blood and the blue puddle. "What about the bodies?"

"One body," said the officer. He jerked a thumb up in the direction of an unpaved side road. "Most of one, anyway."

Through the trees, Tom could see more red and blue lights. He followed the path. A half dozen uniformed cops crawled around the area, some shining flashlights through the nearby thickets. In the center of the clearing was a white sheet covering something large. Tom approached the closest officer to it and flashed his press badge again. This one was short and looked much younger.

"What's the story?" Tom asked.

The officer shook his head. "All we know is the car belonged to him," the young officer gestured towards the sheet. "It started off there," pointing to the overlook, "and tire tracks lead back out to where that car is. My guess is he wasn't driving it."

"How's that?"

"He's..." the young officer paused as if searching for words. "You want to see him?"

Tom nodded gravely. The officer pulled back the sheet. At first, it didn't register what Tom was looking at. When it did, bile rose to his mouth. He recoiled and turned away. The officer laid the sheet back down.

"Looks like the collar bone is all that's holding the two halves of him together," the young officer said.

"Any idea how this could've happened?"

The young officer shook his head. "You beat the coroner here. You'll have to wait for him to say."

"What about whoever left that blood back there?" Tom motioned to the crashed car on the street.

"GODDAMMIT!" a shrill voice cried from that same direction. "Someone want to tell me why the hell we're letting a cheap muckraker crawl around an active crime scene?!" A corpulent blob of a man sauntered into the clearing. He was wearing a uniform as well that appeared a few sizes too small.

Tom immediately felt sorry for the poor buttons straining on that shirt.

"You want to go back to pushing pencils in a cubicle downtown?" the portly man said to the young officer. Even in the flashing lights, Tom could see that the man's jowly face was red. A shock of white hair formed a mustache swimming in all that angry face.

"No, sir, Chief," said the young officer.

"Get this hack out of here," said the Chief.

"Tom Dickens. You must be Chief Stark. I don't believe we've formally met," Tom smiled. He reached his hand for a handshake he knew wasn't coming.

"You could be Shirley-fucking-Temple for all I care. If you don't get outta here right fucking now, I'm booking your ass for obstruction." His beady eyes told Tom it was true.

With a nod, Tom went back to his car. He pulled out his laptop, typed up a quick report for the Online Edition of the paper, and closed the laptop. Then he fired up the car and flipped it around.

This time, Tom obeyed the traffic laws on his way to the office. Sunrise was still a few hours out. Tom passed a few cars on his way down the mountain. Any one of them could have contained the coroner. But probably not the Corvette Stingray purring its way up the mountain road. At least, not unless the coroner had recently had a three-quarter life crisis.

CHAPTER 2
PAULA

THE MIDNIGHT blue Stingray's tires hugged the pavement as the car climbed the steep mountain road. They were guided by a pair of gloved hands that deftly handled the twists and turns.

Paula glanced in the rearview mirror. She was wearing a tan trench coat and a dark fedora. Even in the dark, she preferred to wear shades. She wore knee-high equestrian boots. Her lipstick was fire engine red. When she reached a wall of stopped cars in the right-hand lane, she crossed the double yellow lines and drove against the flow of traffic up the left-hand lane. Not that there was any traffic. The road ahead was certainly blocked.

When she reached the police tape, she parked in the street and got out of the car. A tall uniformed cop raised a hand to stop her.

"Road's closed, ma'am," he said. "No press either," he added.

"Don't sweat it, Jack," she said. "I'm no hack. I'm a shamus. Here on business." She flashed a badge showing she was a licensed private investigator. The tall officer hesitated, then waved her through. She crossed under the tape and pulled out a pen and pad. She let out a low whistle when she looked at the car, splattered with blood.

"What's the story, pops?" she asked, motioning to the wreck.

The tall officer shrugged. "Sometime between two and three AM, somebody hit it hard going backwards. Came from over there." He pointed to a dirt road up ahead. "Body's been ripped in half. Almost."

"That body didn't happen to belong to an eighteen-year-old girl, did it?" Paula said. "That's who I'm looking for."

The tall officer shook his head. "White male. Black hair. Around 5'10". The coroner hasn't shown up yet. We don't have an ID on the body." Paula took notes while the tall officer spoke.

"You don't mind if I take a look at the stiff, do you?" she asked.

"I don't think that's a good idea. The chief's up there now, and he doesn't want any snooping."

"Don't sweat it, Jack. I'll be so fast he won't even know I was here."

The officer opened his mouth to protest, but Paula was already halfway there.

The white sheet over the body glowed eerily in the moonlight. Paula lifted the corner and gagged. From the smell, it was clear the lower intestines had ruptured. She covered her nose and mouth with a handkerchief from her back pocket and tried again. She studied the contorted face pressing into the sandy soil.

"Who the fuck are you?" came a high-pitched rasp from behind.

"Easter bunny," said Paula. "I thought I might have left a few eggs under this sheet."

"Oh, that's cute," Chief Stark said. "JOHNSON! I thought I told you to shore up that line. For fuck's sake, this is a homicide scene! And it's got more holes than a French whore!"

"Don't bust your hernia, Jack," said Paula. She flashed the badge again. "I'm here about a girl. I'm on her folk's dime. They got the idea she might've run off with a guy. Maybe this guy." She motioned to the corpse with her head.

"You might run off and wait for the report this afternoon," Chief Stark said. Then chuckled: "Christ. Hiring a woman as a private dick. Now I've seen everything."

"Bet you ain't seen yours since the Clinton administration," Paula muttered.

"What's that?" said Stark.

"I said I'm sure you boys will have all this figured out before us girls even start cooking our husbands' dinner tonight. I'm blowing this joint."

Stark's face turned a deep red. "You stay the fuck outta this case," he said.

If she'd heard, she didn't show any sign of it. Paula was already walking away.

"Johnson!" yelled Stark. "Escort her out."

The tall officer came up to her. "You heard the Chief," he said. "Let's not make trouble."

"I wouldn't dream of it," she said.

They were almost to the tape that read 'police line-do not cross' (and out of Chief Stark's field of view) when she said, "Oh, one thing! I forgot to grab this license plate number."

The tall officer glanced over his shoulder to see if Stark was looking. "Okay. But be quick about it."

Paula walked over to the wrecked car. The license plate was smashed almost flat against the rocks of the mountain. She had to kneel beside the mangled heap to get a good look. Just then, something caught her eye. It was very small and blinking red.

"Hello," she said. "What do we have here?"

"JOHNSON!" called Stark's shrill voice.

"Hey, lady-" began the officer.

"I'm coming," she said. She pocketed the small object, made a quick note of the plate number, and left under the tape.

Back in her car, she pulled out her phone and dialed.

While it rang, she pulled the blinking red object out of her pocket and examined it. It was a small, flat circle with a half dozen tiny hooks on the bottom. On top was just a small red light blinking in a slow rhythm.

The person on the other end answered the call.

"Hey," she said. "It's me. No sign of her yet. I just found the guy though... No. He's dead... I don't know how. I've got a couple new ends to work. Listen, I'm not going to sugarcoat it. I think she could be in serious trouble. I say we cast a wide net. This thing wouldn't stay under wraps if we tied it up with a steel bow. Besides, that's not going to help us find her now... Uh-huh... yes... Well, here's what I propose. I reach out to the press. They'll be all over this like white on rice anyway. That might kick up something that'll help us find her. And the more people looking for her right now, the better... Report her missing to the fuzz if you want. Off the record, I wouldn't trust the cops in this town to bag my groceries. But then, any resources we can pull help. Okay then. I'll call you when I've got more." She hung up the call.

She chewed her lip for a moment, turning the strange, round device over and over in her gloved hand. Then she dialed another number. It was after hours, but she knew they'd pick up. Sure enough, after three rings, someone picked up.

"Hello... Hi Gladys... Listen, I'm a shamus with dope on a murder case. Let me talk to the big boss over there... yes, I'll hold."

She revved the car and turned it back down the mountain, descending at a steady pace.

A man picked up and introduced himself. "... Hi Dirk. Listen, I'll make this fast. A girl's missing. Gone two days. Name's Rhonda Rhodes. Look her up. She was the dead guy's beau. And I've been hired to find her... Uh-huh... Here's what I want. You give me every-thing you can find on her and her whereabouts, and I'll give you all my dope- exclusive! How about it?... Swell.

Take this number down." She gave her number. "Now, you get anything you bring it to me first. If I find you printing anything I don't know about, deal's off. Savvy?" She hung up.

It was still dark, the moonlight shining down like silver rain. On a sharp turn at the base of the mountain, she cut the wheel hard to the right. Her sleeve hiked up her arm, revealing thick black fur.

CHAPTER 3
TOM

THE ARCHITECTURAL INSPIRATION for The Island Eye newspaper's main (and only) office may well have been a shoebox. The exterior was a sun-bleached tan. The interior was a celebration of dark wood grain and mustard yellow penny tile. If the computers were all replaced with typewriters, one might get the impression they'd stepped through a time portal and landed in 1970.

Though The Island Eye owned the building, half the building was leased to an unrelated staffing agency for office temps. A smaller section was leased to a screen printing company to put logos on mugs and T-shirts. The Eye probably made more leasing out these offices than it did selling papers, Tom had once mused.

The small remaining section still used by the Eye was the only one with lights on at this hour. This is where Tom headed when he arrived.

A couple of bleary-eyed employees were hunched over keyboards on the low-partitioned cubicles of the office floor. Tom stopped off in the break room. He poured himself a Styrofoam cupful of acrid black coffee. Then he headed for the back.

"Good morning, Gladys," said Tom. Gladys's desk sat in front of a door that read 'Dirk Daily- Editor in Chief.'

"Good morning, Tom," she said. It was the earliest in the morning that Tom had ever seen Gladys. Her hair was piled atop her head in a messy bun. She was wearing no makeup, and crow's feet wrinkled in the corner of her eyes as she shone him a sad smile. "You missed a button," she added.

Tom looked down and saw that indeed, one half of his shirt was six inches below the other. He thanked her and corrected it. He remembered he had- indeed- gotten dressed in the dark.

"I read your blurb. It sounds like there was something you couldn't print?" she asked.

"Looks like someone ripped him in half. Whoever had been driving the car either left or got taken away before the cops came. There was some blood around the car, too. I couldn't get much more information. Jolly old Saint Nick wasn't too happy about me nosing around."

Gladys shuddered. "It's just awful. Do you think it was murder?"

"He didn't do it to himself, that's for sure. My guess is whoever crashed the Mustang was getting away from whoever or whatever did THAT. After they crashed, I don't know. Hopefully, the coroner will be able to ID the body soon and we'll have more to go on."

"It's just awful," she repeated. "All this death and murder business. It seems people can't wait to read all about it. Not just to be informed. I mean for kicks!" She sipped her own Styrofoam cup of coffee, light in color from cream and sugar. "Dirk says this'll sell more papers than any issue in the last five years."

Tom nodded. It was probably true.

Gladys narrowed her gaze at him. "Are you taking care of yourself? Still staying at that place?"

"I'm getting by."

"Tom," her voice dropped to a whisper, "it's been six months. Don't you think it's time you put yourself out there? You don't look half bad when you clean up. Meet some girls. Have some dates. It'd be good for you."

"Yeah."

"I mean it, Tom. Moping around won't bring her back."

"I don't want her back, I... Look, I'm fine, Gladys. Really."

The phone on Gladys's desk beeped. She pressed a button and picked up the receiver.

"He'll see you now," she said.

Tom nodded. He swigged the last bit of coffee in his cup and entered Dirk's office.

———

Dirk Daily sat behind a dated rectangular desk that was right at home in the dated rectangular building. The wood-paneled wall behind him was adorned with a beach-themed calendar, plaques, awards, and photos of Dirk shaking hands with people, most of which Tom didn't recognize. Besides the calendar, everything was more than five years old. A plastic ficus gathering dust in the corner struggled to add a pop of cheer to the room.

On the desk, a landline phone was flickering with red and orange lights. (Tom had never once seen Dirk use a cell phone.) Behind the desk sat Dirk- a frenzy of wild energy in human form. By appearances, it was hard to tell if he'd stayed working late or come in very early. His salt and pepper crew cut shot up as if it had been electrified. His bushy eyebrows, still jet black as ever, arched above two striking, if slightly bloodshot, eyes. The sleeves of his white shirt were rolled to the elbows. His red tie hung slack around his unbuttoned collar. His blazer had been discarded on the back of his chair.

Dirk didn't seem to notice Tom. He was transfixed on the ancient computer monitor before him.

"You wanted to see me, Sir?" Tom said.

"Tom!" he said. "Yes! Sit!" Dirk gestured for a chair. "You look like hell."

"Thanks."

"I got your piece from earlier. Christ! This is going to be a media frenzy." Dirk tossed back a cup of coffee. His was in a proper mug. A promotional giveaway mug that bore the logo of a local law firm.

Tom idly wondered if it was printed in the offices next door. "This is going to move more papers than any story Dath Island's seen since those shark attacks in '93." Dirk gazed wistfully at one of the plaques on the wall. "You know about the girl?"

"What girl?"

"What am I paying you for? Look. Just came through." With some effort, Dirk turned the old computer monitor sideways so Tom could see. "Coroner ID'd the body. Kid named Duke Leary. 18. Then there's a report of a girl who didn't come home last night. Rhonda Rhodes. Same age. Same High School."

The picture on the monitor looked as though it came from the High School yearbook. It showed a vivacious girl with intelligent eyes and a bright smile. Even with all the grim stories he'd covered, Tom had a hard time seeing that face in the bloody, chaotic scene on the mountain road. He thought of the bloody crashed car and shuddered.

"Do we know they're connected?"

"We don't. Find out," Dirk slammed back another dram of coffee. "We're running a special edition that goes to print in two hours. I want everything you know and every interesting guess typed, formatted, and on my desk by-" he glanced at his watch. "no later than 5:30. When you're done with that, I'm putting you on finding out everything you can about this girl. Human interest piece."

Tom looked at the face on the screen again before Dick turned the monitor away.

"Now go!" Dirk was already answering his blinking telephone by the time Tom closed the door.

CHAPTER 4
TOM

TOM TYPED UP HIS PIECE. It was a lot of fluff and conjecture to hit the word count, but it was on schedule and he was free to leave.

Tom rubbed his eyes with his fists. It was almost 6:00am. Outside, the first light of dawn was beginning to glow. Gulls squawked overhead as Tom left the Island Eye's main office and crossed the parking lot to his sun eaten car. It looked even worse in the light of day. Then again, he thought rubbing the unshaven stubble on his chin, so did he.

He cranked the car. It wouldn't start. He tried again. Nothing. After a few attempts, he gave up and called a cab.

When the yellow cab pulled up, Tom was ready to collapse into the back seat and sleep. The driver on the other hand was chipper and well rested.

"Where to, boss?" the driver said.

"Duneside Suites. 32nd and Broadway."

"Getting the day started early today, eh?"

Tom grunted.

"You work for the newspaper?"

"Afraid so."

"You heard about what happened last night?"

Tom didn't want to talk about what happened last night right now. Tom just wanted to sleep.

"Sure," Tom said. "How'd you hear about it?"

"On the radio," said the driver cheerily. "There ain't been a murder on old Dath Island in twenty years as best I remember. In fact it's so boring and full of old people, you know what the young kids are calling it, boss? Death Island. Now if that ain't mean, I don't know what is. Used to be kids respected their elders, ain't that right boss? Now I ain't old, but I'm no spring chicken. 59 years young. How many you got under your belt, boss?"

Too many to be having this conversation so early in the morning, Tom wanted to say. "31," he said instead.

"Thirty one?! Aw, you're a young cat yet. You've got the whole world ahead of you. See, I remember a time when this island was just a peaceful little vacation spot. Now it's growing like a weed. Big companies moving in. Cost of living going up. Makes it tough on us little guys, you know? Now we got kids getting killed and going missing. The world sure is getting crazy."

Sitting up was a chore. Tom decided to give it up and stretched out as best he could across the backseat. He and the driver were separated by a metal grate. Tom wished it were soundproof.

Beneath the grate was a small section of ads under a plexiglass panel. Tom distracted himself from the driver's chatter by reading them. Besides, it seemed he was having a fine conversation without Tom's contribution.

Most were promoting touristy activities. There was one for "Wild Werewolf Tours" that took people's money by playing up the local superstition- showing them empty spots where locals said werewolves once did something or other. Tom felt the whole thing was silly and had been glad when, in his early career as a journalist, he was able to stop covering fluff pieces like the annual "werewolf parade" which consisted of a few dozen people and a sad papier-mâché float of a werewolf's head.

Another ad from Brachyura Industries read "Part-time and Full-time work available" and listed minimum wage as the hourly rate. Tom knew the place. In fact, it was located just up the mountain not far from the crime scene he'd visited a few hours ago. The sprawling complex had many detractors among locals for marring the natural beauty of the island. But since it brought jobs and industry to sleepy little Dath Island, it was allowed to operate as it wished.

The ad below that advertised "Scuba Diving-Lessons and Tours with Lisa Lane." Underneath the lettering, a vivacious woman with blonde hair and white teeth beamed at Tom. He wished he felt half as enthusiastic for life as she seemed to.

When the cab pulled into the Dunrise Motel, Tom

imagined falling to his knees and kissing the earth like a sailor returning from a long and perilous voyage. Instead, he paid the driver and climbed on leaden legs up to his second story room. Puko might have said something to him, but he didn't understand or respond. He stumbled through the door, collapsed onto the bed, and fell into a deep dreamless sleep.

CHAPTER 5
BRACHYURA

A SCREECHING roar echoed through the empty halls of the complex as the blast doors whined open. Scuttling feet tapped out a mad Morse code on the sterile floors of the lab.

The inner sanctum of Brachyura Industries was secured by cameras, fingerprint-operated security doors, and a range of special sensors. It had to be. Brachyura Industries maintained strict security due to the highly confidential nature of their work. In the center of the room sat Dr. Braxton Brachyura himself. He was a thin man with white hair combed neatly back, sunken cheekbones, and wore a gray knit turtleneck. He was impassively calm as the dread visage of a mutant crustacean nearly 10 feet tall came lumbering towards him. In its mighty claw hung the limp form of Rhonda Rhodes' body.

The doctor pressed a button on the small remote control in his hand. The beast stopped immediately.

With the press of another button, the creature lowered Rhonda gently down on the cold tile floor.

One side of her face was bruised a bluish violet hue. Her clothes were partly torn. A trickle of blood ran from her nose. The doctor performed a visual scan of her body. In spite of her injuries, she was quite beautiful. He pressed two fingers to her jugular. A strong, steady pulse confirmed she was indeed still alive.

"Very good," he thought to himself.

He took her up in his arms and lifted her easily onto a gurney that had been prepared. He secured her wrists and ankles to the gurney with straps. Rolling the gurney onto the floor scale, he took her weight. He measured out a few CC's of sedative into a small syringe and plunged the needle into her arm. Now he could be assured she would not rouse until he was ready.

Dr. Brachyura now crossed the room and turned his attention to a large screen. The screen showed a map of Dath Island. On the map were two blinking red dots. One of the red dots was here in his lab. The other one seemed to be moving down the mountain into town. Brachyura furrowed his brow.

The blinking dot here in his office made sense. Here was the hulking crab waiting patiently across the room. The other made less sense. He had instructed both creatures to return to his lab. Had one of them willfully disobeyed? The thought irritated him.

His phone rang in his pocket. The caller ID showed it was that butterball of a police chief. Brachyura sighed deeply and answered.

"Talk to me," he said.

"Braxton. It's Stark."

"I know," said Brachyura, shutting his eyes and massaging the bridge of his nose. "What is it?"

"One's dead. Damn near cut in half. The other's missing."

"Yes, I've got her here," said Brachyura. He smiled back at Rhonda bound to her gurney. "Do you have it under control?"

"The press are crawling around this one like flies on shit. We ID'd the stiff. He's a nobody, but he'll draw attention being cut in half and all. Bad news for you. The girl was a runaway. Her folks hired a private dick. A woman, but a shamus no less."

"Are you saying you're incapable of handling the situation?" Brachyura asked.

"Oh, no. I can handle it. Won't be easy though. Didn't know this boy would go through the slicer like that. Might be a bit tough to keep this from blowing back on you. At least for the price we discussed."

"But you can handle it?"

"Sure. It's just that, for the price we discussed-"

Brachyura pulled the phone away from his ear. In that moment he would have paid almost any amount just to get that shrill, raspy voice to stop talking.

"You'll see a deposit in your account tomorrow morning for double our stated rate," Brachyura said. "There'll be additional deposits later for your continued cooperation."

"Sure. I'll just-"

Brachyura hung up and sighed. 'A private investigator?' he thought. The bumbling press didn't shake him in the least, but this rogue element could complicate things. The chief, however much he grated on the doctor's nerves, had proven useful and earned his pay. His non-cooperation with the PI was assured, but still Brachyura despised that which he could not control.

On that thought, he looked up at the blinking red light moving about on his map. If there really was a giant mutant crab menacing downtown as people were waking up to their morning coffee, it'd surely make the news. That was all well and good, but why wasn't it responding? The tests had gone so successfully.

Brachyura used his remote to send the more obedient crustacean back to its tank among a wall of tanks containing a half dozen identical creatures. The doctor's mind was still preoccupied by his non-responsive creation, but that would have to wait. He had other work to attend to. Much more beautiful work to attend to, he thought, looking down at Rhonda's sleeping form.

CHAPTER 6
LISA

THE SMALL BOAT rocked gently on the sea. On the horizon, dawn cast its brilliant fire across the sky. A woman climbed up from below deck and stood at the prow. She was stark naked, and the cool, salty breeze raised goosebumps on her sun-kissed skin and played with her golden locks of hair. She stretched and exhaled a satisfied hum for a good night's rest and the promise of a new day. In one deft, practiced motion, she leapt from prow and dove soundlessly into the water.

The water was warm. It wrapped around her body like a lover's embrace. She paddled a strong breast-stroke until her lungs cried for air and she surfaced. Then, she paddled to the stern and climbed aboard on a small aluminum ladder. The name printed across the hull read "Nauti Gull."

Lisa toweled off. She checked the oxygen tanks and donned a tight wetsuit, fixing her goggles and mouth-piece in place. She grabbed a camera, secured within a clear waterproof housing. And though she had only needed it once in all the years she'd been diving, she strapped her harpoon gun to her back as well. With flippered feet, she plunged back into the briny waters. This time, she was able to look at the magical aquatic world that surrounded her.

Though this had been her morning routine for some time, the ocean never ceased to amaze Lisa. Dath Island was surrounded by some of the clearest waters anywhere in the world. Here, the beautiful coral reefs- a symphony of life in rainbows of color- could be viewed for hundreds of meters in every direction. Anemone waved in the gentle current. Everywhere, schools of brilliant striped fish darted to and fro. From the distance, a soft-shelled sea turtle glided into view. In the wake of mass global pollution, few places on earth could still boast such a magnificent sight.

Lisa aimed the camera at the turtle and snapped several photos as it swam past, nearly close enough that she might have reached out and touched it.

The ocean floor was a few meters below. Lisa descended slowly, adjusting to the increasing pressures of the sea. Though she had explored and photographed much of the reef surrounding the island, there always seemed to be more wonderful secret places hidden beneath the waves. The spirit of adventure pressed her ever onwards.

Here, the ocean floor was covered in magnificent arches and pillars of stone, many of which were festooned with brilliant cup corals and gorgonians.

Angelfish drifted in azure elegance into the scene as if posing for Lisa's pictures. This section of the reef seemed particularly interesting in its diversity of terrain. The ample hiding spots made it a haven for small fish and a hot spot for all manner of aquatic life.

A shifting shadow in Lisa's peripheral vision startled her. She turned, but saw nothing that was cause for alarm. Lisa continued down deeper into the labyrinth of rock and coral below.

She snapped several more photos before a strange sound reached her ears. It was distorted by the water, but it sounded like something hard hitting another hard surface. She looked around. Beneath the waves, the direction of the sound's origin was impossible to identify.

And then she saw it. What had appeared to be another boulder in the rock formations moved. It not only moved, it seemed to move towards Lisa. It approached with frightening speed. Even with all of Lisa's experience with a vast variety of ocean life, she could not identify what this creature might be. Then it raised its arms and spread its claws. Here was the largest crab Lisa had ever seen. And there was no mistake- it was headed straight for her.

The white hot fire of panic shot through Lisa's veins. She kicked with all her might, propelling herself upwards. Perhaps if she could get above the sea floor, she would be out of its grasp. As it drew nearer, Lisa could see that the creature's features were gnarled. Its colors were blotches of red and brown. A sickening, diseased color. Its protruding, inhuman eyes were glazed an icy white. It was now directly beneath her. Impossibly large. The creature lunged upwards and snapped its claws so close to Lisa that the force of it knocked her sideways. She was awash in a maelstrom of dizziness and disorientation. For horrifying moments, she didn't know which way was up.

She was now several meters above the ocean's floor. Her head began to ache, and her muscles began to cramp with the sudden decompression. But adrenaline coursed through her veins, and fear gave wings to her flight. She reached behind her and drew the harpoon gun. A single harpoon sat ready in its shaft. Her muscles were beginning to spasm, and ice picks of pain stabbed her ears. As the monstrous beast lunged once more towards her -its enormous claws open- Lisa took aim and fired a wild shot into the creature's face. A piercing shriek ripped through the water as the harpoon sliced through the creature's eye, ripping it from its socket.

Lisa swam upwards for all she was worth. The dark shadow of the boat above seemed to drift farther away the harder she kicked, the expanding hallways of a fever dream. The pain in her ears was unbearable. Her legs struggled to respond, and a cloud of blood began to pour from her nose. With a desperate kick, she broke through to the world of air. She grasped the ladder and pulled her leaden body upwards. A tug from below yanked her downwards into the water once more. The creature grasped her flipper in its claw.

With a frenzied kick, she dislodged her foot from the

flipper and broke the surface once again. With a single motion, she clambered up the ladder and rolled onto the deck.

The boat leaped into the air with a sudden impact from below. Lisa was tossed wildly and knocked hard against the gunwale. Unstrapping the heavy tank from her back, she rolled herself into the cockpit.

A spray of water erupted from the stern as a giant claw reached up and grasped the ship's stern. The prow tipped upwards, pointing high into the sky. Lisa turned the key and gunned the engine to full throttle. The propeller sprang to life, slicing through the creature's shell. Blue blood and ocean water sprayed across the deck. The prow dropped down level with the horizon again. The boat sped off towards the open sea. And Lisa collapsed in a heap on the floor of the cockpit, gasping for breath.

CHAPTER 7
MAYOR

THE POLICE STATION was already a buzz of activity when Mayor Sam Reams burst through the double doors, accompanied by several camera flashes from one of the unpaid interns working with his re-election campaign. It was important that the mayor was shown taking charge to get to the bottom of this. The mayor wore his red hair in a side part that presided over his red eyebrows and red push-broom mustache. He wore a sandy colored blazer, white slacks, white shoes, and a tastefully understated brown tie with a palm tree barely visible in its design. It would make a dramatic photo indeed.

"Where's Stark?" he asked the receptionist, whose hair was still dancing from the breeze of the mayor's dramatic entrance.

"Back there," said the receptionist, pulling the phone receiver away from their ear and pointing with the blunt end of a pen.

Without another word, Mayor Reams charged off in that direction. His intern followed along with his camera at the ready. The chief was looming above an officer's desk on an open floor of desks in the small police precinct.

"Stark!" bellowed Mayor Reams. "I need a word with you!"

The chief's moonish face did little to disguise his annoyance. He ended his conversation with the desk officer and then addressed the mayor. "My office," he said. The mayor and his intern began to follow the chief. "Not you," the chief said, leveling a meaty finger at the intern. The young man appeared crestfallen. The mayor shot him a glance but said nothing as he followed Chief Stark through the frosted glass door.

The police chief landed heavily in his groaning office chair.

"Have a seat, Sam," he said, motioning to a seat in front of his desk. The mayor sat down. He leaned forward in his chair, grasping the armrests as though he was a coiled spring ready to leap across the desk at the slightest provocation.

"Dammit, Jonas! I want to know what the hell is going on. I slept like a baby last night. Not a care in the world. Today I wake up to a missing girl and the first homicide this island's had in twenty goddam years. I hear this poor son of a bitch was ripped open like a bag of chips- now that's a first ever! And all this just three weeks until the election. I want some goddam answers!

I want to know what the hell you're going to do about it!"

"Sam," said Stark, who'd been sitting patiently through the mayor's rant, "we've known each other a long time. The fuck do you think I'm doing here? Camping out, roasting weenies? We've pooled all our resources to sort this shit out. The girl's a floozy and the guy's a dropout. Couple of nobodies, BUT-" the chief raised a hand to silence a remark from the mayor, "regardless, every available officer in the Dath Island PD is on the case."

The mayor took a deep breath and relaxed his grip on the chair.

"Sorry, Joe," he said. "I just... you know how things are right now. Elections are coming up, and so are the holidays. We've got to have a good tourist season this fall. Overnight, this place looks about as friendly a tourist spot as Whitechapel during the Autumn of Terror."

"C'mon now, Sam," the chief said. He shook his head, jowls jiggling softly.

"No, it's true. The one reason voters like me is that I've raised tourism. A proven track record. I'm ahead in the polls, but not so much that a stain like this couldn't pull the rug out from right under my feet." He snapped his fingers. "Tourism on this island is like floods on the Nile. It's all that keeps us fertile and operating in the black."

"There's the mill on the hill now," said Stark.

"Brachyura Industries," Sam frowned. "I never liked that spot. The council might have liked it because they got dollar signs in their eyes. Taxes. But you know something? How many employees are working up there? 20? 30? They're still operating on a tax credit for another three goddam years. Meantime, I've got a campaign, and the people want tourists. How are we supposed to attract tourists when we go around replacing pristine tropical paradise with some industrial abomination on display on the mountain top like a goddam flag?!"

The chief was silent for a long moment, his hands folded on the table.

"Are you done, Sam?" the chief said at last. "I've got an operation to run."

"Yeah," said Sam. He turned to leave, pausing with his hand on the doorknob before exiting. "Just one more thing." He dropped his voice to a whisper. "There's hell of a lot on the line right now, and I need to come out looking good. You need to hang it on somebody-anybody- so long as it sticks until the election's through, I'll make sure to give you a big thank you if you catch my drift."

Chief Stark winked. The mayor opened the door, revealing a young blonde woman in a wetsuit strolling down the hall.

CHAPTER 8
TOM

A LOUD BANGING catapulted Tom rudely awake from his deep, velvety sleep. Gripped with panic, he shot upright. Then he realized it was someone knocking at the door. He looked at the clock. He'd slept for maybe 15 minutes.

He staggered towards the door.

"Who is it?" he asked.

"The ghost of Christmas Past," came a muffled voice.

Tom opened the door. The bright sunlight stabbed his eyes. As they adjusted, he saw a beautiful woman dressed in a trench coat and fedora leaning against the railing before his door.

"Yikes," she said. "They oughta make you into banana bread."

"What do you want?" asked Tom.

"Same as you," said the woman. She held out a photo that Tom recognized. Rhonda Rhodes. "Her folks hired me to find her. My name's Paula Daschiell." She returned the photo to the breast pocket inside her coat, Tom's eyes sleepily following. "Up top, Jack. That is your beat, right? Chercher la femme?"

"Yeah," said Tom. "How'd you find me?"

"'Cause I'm good at my job," said Paula. "I figured I'd see what you knew. Finding any clues at the bottom of the bottle?" she asked, peering in at the empty cans in the disheveled room.

Tom shut the door a little more. "Listen, my car broke down-"

"I know. I saw it," said Paula. "You took a cab. Why'd you come here instead of going someplace where you might learn something?"

"To sleep," said Tom.

"To sleep?!" she said. "You know right this minute the girl's missing and in who knows what kind of trouble. Her boyfriend's been murdered. And all you can think about is your beauty rest? You call yourself a reporter?"

"Who the hell do you think you are? I AM a reporter!" said Tom.

"Then tell me something I don't know."

Tom stood slack-jawed. He had nothing to say.

"You make me sick," Paula said. She turned to walk off down the walkway.

"Hey," said Tom. "Where are you going?"

"The cop shop."

"Cop shop?" said Tom.

"Yeah, the station." She was still walking away.

"Hang on," said Tom. "Can you give me a lift?"

"Give you a lift?!" said Paula, turning to face him. "Why should I?"

"I can help," he answered.

"Ha! That's a laugh. You couldn't help a fish get wet."

Tom puzzled at this for a moment, then shook it off.

"Hey, two heads are better than one. I... look, things have been rough for me lately, but I am a good reporter. Honest. And you're right. It sounds like she's in trouble. I do want to help."

Paula bit her lip and folded her arms. She seemed to be considering it.

"I don't carry dead weight," she said.

"I won't be," said Tom.

Paula sighed.

"I came here because I've got this crazy idea about old school newspaper journalism being an honorable profession," she said. "Prove me right."

"Alright," Tom said. He grabbed his laptop, shut the door, and raced down the stairs. They both piled into the blue Stingray. Paula brought it roaring to life. They pulled out of the parking lot and merged onto the street.

CHAPTER 9
LISA

THERE HAD BEEN no time to change, so Lisa was still wearing her wetsuit as she burst through the doors into the Dath Island police department.

The receptionist's eyes widened when she approached the desk.

"Can I help you, ma'am?" asked the receptionist.

"I need to see Office Rob Reed," Lisa said. "It's urgent."

"What's this regarding?" asked the receptionist.

"Tell him it's about crabs!" said Lisa.

"I beg your pardon?" said the receptionist.

"Please! It's very important," said Lisa.

The receptionist looked over the barefoot woman in a wetsuit while considering how best to proceed. She was spared the decision when Officer Rob approached the front desk.

"Lisa?" said Rob. "I saw you from across the room.

What are you doing here? And why are you wearing that wetsuit?"

"Rob!" she said, throwing her arms around him. "There's something in the water. It was enormous! A crab. It tried to kill me. I-"

Rob looked around. He could feel everyone on the station's main floor staring at the two of them.

"Hey, take it easy," Rob said. "Let's go find some place to talk about it." Then to the receptionist. "If anyone asks, I'll be back in ten."

Rob led Lisa to a small break room with two tables and a half dozen chairs. He took a seat and motioned for her to do the same.

"All right, darling. Let's start at the beginning. What happened?"

Lisa took a deep breath.

"This morning I went diving. I was taking some pictures of the reef off Craggy Point. All of a sudden, something huge came after me. It was... some kind of awful crab."

"A crab attacked you?" Rob asked.

"Yes," said Lisa. "But not just any crab. This one was HUGE! Like the size of a truck!"

Rob narrowed his eyes but said nothing.

"I managed to get away, but it grabbed onto my boat," Lisa continued. "The propeller chopped off its arm. It was too heavy to bring here, but I still have it. I- I didn't want to call because I knew they'd think I'm crazy. But I have proof! I didn't know who else to come to. This thing is dangerous! I don't know if there are others." Lisa stopped now to catch her breath.

"*Ahem*," Rob cleared his throat. "Well, that's, uh... are you hurt?"

"No. My head is screaming from the decompression, but that thing didn't hurt me." She gazed over at the vending machine as if lost in a deep reverie.

Rob let out a big breath and rubbed his eyes. "What a day. I'm glad you're alright. I'd take a look now, only I'm tied up along with everyone else working on this big case."

"Case?" said Lisa, snapping back to the present. "What case?"

"You haven't heard? Last night a kid was murdered up in the mountains. It was a real mess. He was torn apart. There was a runaway girl who was with him- the lab ID'd her blood left at the scene."

"Do you...? Do you think she killed him?" Lisa asked.

"I doubt it," Officer Rob shook his head. "From the nature of the injuries-"

"REED!" Chief Stark snarled. He flung open the door. "The fuck is this, social hour?!"

"Sorry, Chief." Rob stood and put on his hat.

"I had to report something," Lisa started.

"Then phone it in or fill out a form up front," said the Chief. "We're up to our goddam eyeballs without some skirt strutting around in a wetsuit."

"I'll call you later," said Rob to Lisa. Then he exited.

"You too. Out!" said Stark.

Lisa rose uneasily. The chief gave her a look that could curdle milk as she walked out into the lobby.

CHAPTER 10
TOM

TOM'S PHONE rang in his pocket. He pulled it out and answered. "Tom here."

"Tom," said an excited, familiar voice. "It's Dirk. Your car's in the parking lot. The hell's going on? What's the update?"

Tom glanced over to Paula in the driver's seat.

The Stingray was tearing its way towards downtown. Paula punched it through a yellow light as it turned to red. A car honked at them.

"I'm on the way downtown. I'm getting a lift to the police station. I think I can get more information there."

"We got a call earlier. Some detective looking for the Rhodes girl. She may reach out to you," said Dirk.

"I've met her," said Tom as the Stingray whipped around a corner, knocking him sideways.

"Good," said Dirk. "Listen, these issues are selling like hotcakes. Going to run another special edition tonight. Need you to have a story ready by three.."

Tom glanced at his watch.

"Okay," he said. "It's tight, but I think I can do it."

"Attaboy," said Dirk. "Get at it." He hung up.

Tom braced himself against the dashboard as the car merged, shooting a narrow gap between two cars, leaving mere inches of clearance on either side.

"Jesus!" said Tom. "Careful."

"Mind your knitting grandma," said Paula. She turned the wheel, and the car drifted onto the shoulder, passing a line of cars stopped at the light. The nose lurched hard to the right. The tires screamed against the asphalt. "I aim to get there before Dath's Finest muck this thing up but good."

"You don't have a lot of faith in the police?" said Tom.

"The police?" she laughed. "They're as crooked as a box of fish hooks and less fun to stick your hand in. I've got more faith in the tooth fairy tipping diamonds." She honked at a car attempting to merge into the lane.

"You worked with them before?" asked Tom.

"Say," she smiled, "you may be a reporter yet. Yeah, I've worked with them, alright. Even managed to solve a few cases in spite of 'em. How about you?"

"Just the usual. Nothing major," said Tom. "I've only been living here about a year now," he added.

"Where from?" said Paula, slamming on the brakes to skid to a halt before almost rear-ending a semi.

"Los Angeles," said Tom.

"LA, huh?" said Paula. "There's got to be a lot more

to report on in the city of angels than this old retirement rock."

"There was," he said.

"So, why'd you move here?"

"My wife," said Tom. "My ex-wife, actually."

"Ah..." said Paula. "I sense a story in that."

"Not too much," said Tom. "She wanted to live on an island, get out of the city. I didn't want to at first, but after she asked enough times, I said okay."

"Hmm. That Band-Aid didn't work long, did it? I don't see any ring line on your finger."

Tom looked down at his hand.

"Forget it," Tom said. "What about you?"

"What about me?" asked Paula.

"I mean, what's your story? Doesn't seem like there's a lot of detective work on sleepy little Dath Island."

"My story's easy," said Paula. "I've been here a long time. I've been a shamus for as long as it's worth remembering."

"I sense a few stories in that," said Tom.

"You'd better believe it, Jack," said Paula. "And the moral of the story is this: when I go after something, I make good. I've seen what people can do to each other. Evil things. I've been stabbed, shot, and had my head kicked in more than once. And I consider myself lucky. You'd be surprised, but I've sniffed out a lot of cases over the years. And I tell you this one stinks. I knew it the minute I saw that smashed Mustang and that poor kid's body popped like a zit. This Rhodes girl is in serious trouble, and come hell or high water, I'm gonna find her. Look, we're here."

She pulled the Stingray into the parking lot of the police station and parked it close to the front.

"How do you mean it stinks?" asked Tom.

"If you've got a conscience and a brain, that's what you'll help me find out. Now hang on a second, I've got to make a call."

Paula pulled out her phone and dialed a number. While it rang, she produced a small round object from her trench coat pocket. It was a dark plastic housing with what appeared to be small metal claws and a red blinking light.

"Does this look familiar to you?" she asked Tom while waiting for someone to answer on the other end of the line.

"No," Tom shook his head. "I've never seen anything like it."

"I know someone who might," said Paula. "Only he doesn't believe in answering machines." She disconnected the call.

"You don't just want to knock on his door and wake him up," Tom smiled.

"Might have to," she said. "Come on. Let's go."

CHAPTER 11
BRACHYURA

THE PHONE RANG in Dr. Braxton Brachyura's pocket. The caller ID showed a turkey emoji. It was the Police Chief calling from his cell phone. Brachyura sighed and answered.

"Yes?" said Brachyura.

"Someone's seen one," said the Chief.

"Where?" said Brachyura. He pulled up the screen that displayed the island map with its one blinking dot.

"Some broad in a wetsuit came down to the station. Says she was attacked by one off Craggy Point. Ripped its arm off with a boat propeller sounds like."

"Hmm. Interesting," said Brachyura.

"You want her followed?" asked Stark.

Brachyura considered this for a moment.

"No," he said. "The town will see them soon enough. Tonight as a matter of fact."

"Tonight, eh? Doesn't that seem a bit... soon?"

Normally, this would have annoyed Brachyura

getting unsolicited advice from his hired help. But his mind was elsewhere, barely present with the offensive chief anymore.

"Not at all," Brachyura said. "In fact, it's perfect. They're all shaken up and ready to be..." The word "shocked" came to mind but he realized he was explaining more than he wished. "You just keep up your end of things."

"Anything I should be prepared for?" Stark said.

"The unexpected," said Brachyura. He disconnected the call. He was staring at the screen again. Based on the position of the blinking red dot, the rogue crab should be walking in the police station's front door. Strange.

Behind him, a row of glass and steel tanks bubbled.

The figures of enormous crustaceans wavered in the distorted light.

Brachyura turned his attention back to the cold steel and tile room in the corner of the private lab.

The door opened with a pneumatic hiss. Inside, Rhonda lay bound by hands and feet to a bed. A gag was in her mouth. Her eyes rolled beneath half-open lids.

"I see you're waking up," said Brachyura. "That's good. You have a strong life force. But we're not quite ready yet."

Brachyura went to a small sterile table in the corner of the room containing various surgical instruments—scalpels, sutures, and the like. He loaded another syringe with clear liquid from a small glass bottle.

Rhonda looked towards him, her eyes still only half

open. A small, choked groan issued from her mouth around the gag.

"I like a girl with spirit," said Brachyura. "If only for the challenge of breaking it."

He crossed the room and brought the needle to her arm. Her eyes widened. She strained against her restraints and against the drugs that turned her arms and legs into heavy concrete blocks.

"Now hold still," said Brachyura. "It will be very painful for you if I miss the vein."

He grabbed her with his smooth, well-manicured hands. He easily stilled her arm and plunged the needle into her, squeezing the liquid into her blood.

Her eyes rolled back in her head.

Brachyura felt her go limp. A satisfied smile spread across his thin face. He smoothed back the hair that had fallen over her forehead and planted a small kiss. Then, exiting the room he strode over to the tanks of enormous crabs.

The creatures perched in their tanks. They were dormant for now but ready for action at a moment's notice.

"Tonight is your big night," he said softly to the crabs. Then another thought rushed in that brought a still bigger smile to him. "Tonight is *my* big night! Tonight will live forever in history."

CHAPTER 12
DATH ISLAND - 1625

THE FULL MOON *shone brightly over the bay. The waves reflected its light and the undulating contours of its surface. Gentle waves crashed on the glowing sand and hissed back into the ocean. A warm breeze shifted the palm fronds lazily about on the coast.*

Overhead, an infinite expanse of stars hung like a magical cloak over the earth, melding seamlessly with the watery horizon. Even in the darkness, the primordial beauty of the island flowers was impossible to ignore. Some were the size of dinner plates. The scene was one of quiet tropical beauty.

In the middle distance, a sailing boat sat anchored offshore. Approaching from this direction, two whitewashed dinghies drifted into view. Each carried a half dozen men. Their white skin had been tanned like leather from seafaring lives in the harsh tropical. Their sunken eyes fixed on the island or flitted nervously about to one another silently.

They dipped their oars carefully into the water, taking care not to splash. A thirteenth figure sat solemnly in the center of one boat. His skin was much darker, even more than the suntanned men surrounding him. His hands were tightly bound with a rough length of rope that bit painfully into his wrists. He wore a grass skirt and a necklace of seashells hung around his muscular neck. The white man behind him held a blunderbuss, its cold metal barrel pressed into the dark man's back.

"Nae tricks now," said the captor to the dark man. "Ye jus kip quiet lest yer spoken tuh. Izzat clear?"

The dark man nodded silently as the gun pressed harder into his back.

The surf slapped the sides of the ship, spraying drops of briny water against the dark man's bare flesh. The prow of the boat hissed against the sand. The frontmost man slipped quietly over the prow and pulled the boat further up onto the beach. Quietly, the white men stepped off the boat into the knee-deep surf. They held their flintlock rifles overhead, taking care to keep their gunpowder dry. Most had empty rucksacks slung over their shoulders and long daggers secured to their belts.

"Yer turn," said the man with the blunderbuss to the dark man. "Oot. And be quiet aboot it."

The dark man stepped his bare feet over the gunwale and over the starboard side. The briny water stung his cuts. The white man with the blunderbuss had a rope tied around his waist, the other tied to the dark man's wrists. He followed the dark man onto the shore, keeping the gun leveled squarely at him.

The men were gathering on the shore and checking the powder in their guns and the sharpness of their blades when one of them raised a hand and shushed the crowd.

"D'ya hear tha?" he said.

The men strained their ears against the warm night breeze. Faintly, a rhythmic knocking sound pulsed from somewhere down the beach.

"Drums," said one of them.

"Aye," said another. He drew his saber from its sheath. "Comin' from thatta way."

"Let's go," said one wearing a three-pointed hat with a sad, worn-out feather tucked in its band. The dark man took this white man to be their leader. "Keep silent and keep your wits about you."

The crowd began to move down the beach towards the drumming sound. A firm hand shoved the dark man rudely forward, nearly throwing him off his feet.

"Walk," said the captor. The dark man obeyed.

The men's bare feet and hobnailed boots were nearly silent on the sand. The sound of chirping insects rose and fell. And the drumming became louder as they approached. It seemed to get into the dark man's blood. His heartbeat quickened until it began to match the pounding drums. A film of fear and sweat coated his skin.

"Aagh!" came a cry from behind. The whole party turned. They saw the man at the rear lift a dark snake from off his shoulder and throw it to the ground. He swung his sword down and clove the snake in half, its blood trickling into the sand. The man stood breathing heavily. Everyone paused to listen. The drums continued to beat uninterrupted.

"You fool!" said the man in the three-pointed hat. It was a

harsh whisper through gritted teeth. "I should hang you from the nearest yardarm with your own yellow guts!"

"But sir, I-"

"But nothing!" said the hatted man. "Up front where I can keep an eye on you."

The party moved forward down the beach. The drums grew close enough that the reverberations echoed in the men's chests. It stood the hair of their arms on end. Now, yellow fire peaked through the dense foliage. Voices could be heard chanting and wailing above the drums.

The party waded into the thick foliage beyond the tree line. The approach was slowed, but carried inexorably forward to the rhythm of the drums. They climbed a small ridge and looked down upon the source of the sound.

A great bonfire blazed in a clearing, surrounded by a dozen huts. The drummers could be seen beating their instruments furiously. Around the fire men, women, and children leapt and danced, bare to the waist with grass skirts flying wildly about. Many wore masks and head ornaments. They waved spears above their heads with heavy obsidian points glistening in the fire's flicking glow. Their wails were anguished and raw, sending shivers up the white men's spines. In the middle of it all by the fire, a woman with a covered head was lashed to a thick tree. Her large breasts were bare and she wriggled against her restraints.

"Jesus," said on of them. "Thar mus be two score of em doon thar."

"What are they saying?" the man in the hat asked the dark man. The dark man knew the chant well. It brought fear to his heart. He did not know the white man's words for what it meant. Even if he had, he knew he would not say.

"They pray for good weather," said the dark man. "For the storms to stay away."

"And what about that one?" he said, pointing to the masked woman tied to the tree.

"Sacrifice," said the dark man.

"Heathens," scoffed the captor, bound with rope to the dark man.

"Is there food in those huts?" asked the hatted man.

The dark man nodded.

"Alright," said the hatted man. "You six circle that way. Cut off their retreat. The rest of you follow me."

The captor shoved the dark man to follow the hatted man's party down the hillside through the thick underbrush towards the bonfire. The hatted man led the way to the edge of the clearing, mere yards from the epicenter of the nocturnal rites. The hatted man raised his fist and the company gathered quietly behind him.

"Fix bayonets," he said. When this was done, he continued. "Our mates should be in position now. Prepare to fire the first volley on my signal."

The captor untied the rope from his waist and tied it to a nearby palm tree. Perspiration beaded on the dark man's face as he anticipated the scene to follow. His eyes were fixed on the wriggling woman who was lashed to the tree.

"They ne'er hae seen these, eh boy," the captor asked the dark man, motioning to his gun. The dark man shook his head, but didn't shift his gaze.

The white men lifted their flintlocks to their shoulders and took aim at the dancing crowd. The chants seemed to grow louder. The drumbeats quickened.

"FIRE!" yelled the hatted man.

Thunder and smoke erupted from the muzzles of a dozen guns. The dark captive tried to cover his ears with his bound hands. Musket balls ripped through the flesh of the men and women of the island. Screams tore through the night.

"CHARGE!" came the next order.

The white men poured forth from the trees with battle cries into the clearing. The locals, caught off guard, were stuck with swords and bayonets. Red blood soaked the sand. From where he was tied, the dark man saw in the clearing musket smoke a child lying dead in the bonfire glow.

The natives running for the treeline were met by the second party and hacked down by cruel steel blades. A spear sailed through the air, impaling one of the invading sailors in the throat, a fountain of blood pouring from his jugular vein. This was the only casualty on the attacker's side.

The dark man could see at least seven natives lying dead or dying on the ground.

"Quickly," said the hatted man. "Raid the food stores and reload before they regroup."

A group of the invaders pillaged the huts. The man who had been the captor approached the woman who was still lashed to the tree and pulling with all her might against the ropes.

"Well now," he said. "A flow'r of paradise, an' all wrapped up tah boot." He ran his dirty hands up the bare skin of her breasts. "Eets been ah long time since I known the comp'ny uf a womin."

He drew his dagger and cut the ropes that bound her to the tree.

A scream caught in the dark man's throat as he watched helplessly from the tree where he himself was tethered.

The rope around the woman came loose, and she sprang forth from her bonds with shocking speed. Her fingernails were long claws that lashed out at the man who'd cut her down, slicing his belly. Rubbery intestines and blood spill forth onto the sand. Naked horror spread across his face and his hands reached uselessly to contain the spilling organs.

The woven mask was still upon her head as she bounded toward the nearest man loading his musket. She tore the mask from her head, revealing a long mouth filled with sharp fangs, twinkling in the fire's glow. The man's scream was cut short when she pounced upon him and tore into the man's throat with her fangs, ripping it from his neck with a swift jerk of her head.

A musket shot whizzed over her head. She bounded into the tree line.

The dark man's breath verged now on hyperventilation. A paroxysm of dread seized him when a hand fell upon his shoulder. He looked behind him to see a man of his tribe, with a finger pressed against his lips for silence. The man produced an obsidian knife from his belt and cut the cord that bound the captive. Together the two of them ran inland, deeper into the forest.

"Cap'n Dath! Cap'n Dath!!!" cried one of the white men from the clearing behind, followed by the screams of men being ripped apart beneath the full moonlight.

CHAPTER 13
TOM

PAULA AND TOM mounted the concrete steps to the heavy wooden doors of the police station. With a gloved hand, Paula gripped the big brass handle and pulled it open. Tom followed directly behind.

"Here's the plan," said Paula. "I'll shake down the boys to see what I can find out. You keep an eye out for anything suspicious."

Just then a short blonde woman in a wetsuit came walking past on her way out. Paula and Tom exchanged a glance and turned towards her. Paula gestured towards the woman with her head.

"Excuse me," called Tom after the woman in the wetsuit.

She turned to face him. Her eyes were red and tears rolled down her cheeks.

"Yeah?" she sniffed.

"Listen, I'm sorry to bother you like this, but I- we" he gestured to Paula, "are running down a missing girl by the name of Rhonda Rhodes. You wouldn't happen to know anything about it would you?"

"No," she said. "I heard something about it just now. But no. I don't know anything."

"Is everything okay?" Tom said. "I'm sorry. My name's Tom. Tom Dickens. This is Paula Daschiell."

He reached out his hand to shake her. When she grabbed his hand, he was surprised by her strength. Her skin wasn't smooth, but it wasn't rough either. A certain electricity seemed to flow from it into his.

"Nice to meet you, " said Paula.

"I'm Lisa. And thanks for asking," she said. "Say, Tom Dickens? Where have I heard that name before..."

"He's a hack for the local rag," said Paula.

"That's it!" said Lisa. "You write for the newspaper." Her features lifted as a smile began to grow across her face.

"That's me," said Tom. "It's not often I meet someone who's read my work. At least anyone under 60."

She laughed.

"I don't read the paper much. But I never watch the news. It's so crowded with lies and filler it's hard to find anything true," she said. "Say, it's lucky I bumped into you."

"Why's that?" asked Tom.

"I just tried to report something, but I don't think the police will take it seriously."

"What is it?" asked Paula.

"It's going to sound hard to believe- in fact, here.

Look at this," she said. She reached into the bag slung over her shoulder and produced a large digital camera in a waterproof housing. "The picture's small, but... There!" She had pulled up a photo on the camera's tiny screen.

"What are we looking at?" asked Tom.

"That," she pointed "is the stern of my boat! And this is blood."

Tom squinted at the tiny picture. Sure enough, it was the stern of a boat. It was badly battered.

"You mean those blue puddles?" asked Paula, her eyes widening.

Lisa nodded emphatically.

"What did this?" asked Tom.

"A giant crab," said Lisa.

"Giant crab?" said Tom incredulously.

"Yes," Lisa nodded again. "I told you it's hard to believe, but I saw it. I was diving and it came out of nowhere and attacked me. It almost killed me! I just filed a paper report, but I don't think it will do much good. Maybe- maybe if we put it in the paper someone will listen. It's too dangerous to let people go out on the beach when it's running around. It's DEADLY!"

"How big would you say this giant crab was?" asked Paula.

"Oh! It was big. Maybe the size of a minivan."

Paula bit her lip and paused. Then said, "Cool it here a minute, Cousteau. Tom, step into my office, will ya?"

She led Tom to a corner of the lobby.

Lisa grabbed one arm with the other and waited by the door.

"What do you think?" Paula asked Tom when they were out of earshot.

"I mean that blue blood looks a lot like the stuff at the scene of the crash," said Tom. "It sounds crazy though."

"It does," Paula shook her head. "But in a screwy way, it makes me think. If there was a crab that size and it got a hold of somebody-"

"-that it could pinch them almost in half," Tom finished.

"Bingo," said Paula.

"How should we do this?" asked Tom. "Are we both going to go check it?"

Paula thought for a moment, then shook her head.

"You check it out," she said. "I'm going to work another lead. You call me if you learn something useful." She handed Tom a business card. Tom placed it in his wallet.

"Okay," he said. "Thanks." He headed back over to Lisa. "What happened to that crab?"

"After he wrecked the back of my boat, I turned on the propeller and cut off his arm. I guess it was a 'he' anyway."

"Does your boat still run? I mean, do you think you can take me to the spot where it happened? Maybe we can find the arm. Then we'll have some proof."

"Sure, I can take you there," she said. "I don't know

if there are any others, but if it's still alive even with one arm, that thing is dangerous."

"That's okay," said Tom. "Somehow, I think this crab and Rhonda have something to do with each other." He paused for a moment. "Do you have a car?"

"Sure," she said. "I'll give you a lift."

"Let's go," said Tom.

He turned back to wave goodbye to Paula, but she was already gone.

CHAPTER 14
TOM

AS IT TURNED OUT, Lisa's car was a cherry red Volkswagen Beetle with plastic flower outlines covering the taillights. A plush teddy bear grinning and holding a plush heart dangled from the rear-view mirror. The floorboards were covered in detritus- gum wrappers, plastic bottles, what appeared to be a condom wrapper, and other unidentifiable junk. Lisa had to move a crumpled pile of clothes from the passenger seat and throw them in the backseat before Tom had a place to sit. An empty can of seltzer water occupied the cup holder and was covered in ashes. The interior smelled of a perfume that might have been jasmine covering over smoke. Lisa made no comment about the condition of the car. She put it in reverse, whipped her hair around to face back, and off they went.

The morning rush had ended, but the traffic was still steady. They drove through the quaint pedestrian section of downtown. Palm trees grew in the medians of the main roads. Here were shops renting out bikes with names like "Island Rides" and surf shops like "Hang Ten" and "Big Wave." Some shops peddled useless "Dath Island" knick-knacks- everything from T-shirts and keychains to snow globes and stainless steel coffee mugs. The ways of separating tourists from their money seemed endless.

There weren't too many tourists strolling the streets now as Lisa turned the Beetle down 4th Street heading towards the ocean. Most of the thin crowd sported white hair, sun visors, and the occasional walker. A few panhandlers stood or sat dejectedly in intersections flying signs. One read "Repent! The end is nigh!"

It was nearly noon now and the sun was reaching its apex. It stung Tom's eyes. A headache was beginning to chisel softly at his skull as the previous night's alcohol was beginning to leave his system. Partly to distract himself and partly because it needed doing, Tom whipped out his laptop and began typing up his story of Rhonda Rhodes for the afternoon's special edition of the Island Eye.

"Why do you do it?" asked Lisa, breaking the silence. It took Tom by surprise.

"What do you mean?" he asked.

"Write for the paper?" she said. "I mean, I read it sometimes but most people don't. Most people watch the news on TV or go online. Mostly it's just old people who read the papers."

They drove past a small park where a shaky septuagenarian threw bread crumbs at pigeons from a public bench.

"Fortunately," said Tom, "we live in a place where the average age is about room temperature."

"Yeah," Lisa laughed. "But you're dodging me. I mean, old people still watch the news. Why do you write?"

Tom looked up from his laptop and took a deep breath before answering.

"You know, in all the years I've been doing it, nobody ever once asked me why. Maybe I never really asked myself. Maybe I never really sat down and asked myself."

"No time like the present," said Lisa.

"Yeah," said Tom, rubbing his chin. The stubble there reminded him he still hadn't shaved today. Now with Lisa, he felt embarrassed by his disheveled appearance, but there wasn't much he could do about it now.

"I guess if I had to say," he continued, "it's just how it comes out. I don't know quite what 'it' is. Just whatever is in me that's got to get out, it just wants to come out that way. Like, the words on a page are special. People are like icebergs- most of the truth about them is below the surface. When you watch something, it's like talking to them. You still only see the tip. There's a lot left unseen. But when you read it's different. Nobody's giving you the images. You've got to look at these little symbols somebody put down on the page and make all the pictures and meaning in your own mind. It's like I'm using the page as a middleman to put what's in my brain in some Zip file for your brain to unzip, at their own pace. Maybe it's not perfect, but it makes you think. It makes you consider. So much of our communication is surface-level- so shallow. I guess I believe these stories- these things that happen to real people- deserve more than that." Tom paused and gazed out the window.

"Wow!" said Lisa. "I don't know what I was expecting, but it wasn't that. That was beautiful."

"Thanks," said Tom. "You know, I'd kind of forgotten that piece of it. There's been a lot of soft news and fluff since I moved to the island last year. A whole lot of nothing. Now it seems like everything is happening all at once."

"Whew," said Lisa. "You can say that again. Are you married?"

The question caught Tom by surprise.

"No," he said. "Divorced, actually."

"Oh, I'm sorry," she said.

"Why do you ask?"

"No reason," she said. "Just curious. You seem like someone a girl would want to marry."

Tom laughed. That was a new one.

"What about you?" he asked.

"No," said Lisa. "I've never been married."

"Are you seeing anybody?"

"Eh, sort of," she answered. "I've been dating this guy named Rob, but it's not going so great."

"Why's that?"

"Hey, this isn't going to make it into one of your stories, is it?" Lisa smiled.

Tom smiled back.

"No," he said. "Just personal curiosity."

Lisa sighed."He's always blowing me off. I just went to see him as a matter of fact, to tell him about how I almost DIED a couple of hours ago and it seemed like he couldn't care less. It's been like that."

"Sorry to hear it," said Tom.

The red Volkswagen pulled into the parking lot near the docks. The parking brake made a crunching sound as Lisa pulled it into place. Tom looked at the dappled sunlight playing across the gentle contours of her face and making a fiery halo of her golden hair. A tear welling in the corner of her eye caught the midday light. He could see the hurt and pain in her features, the abandonment she must have felt in the downturned corners of her lips. In that moment, Tom was gripped with an overwhelming urge. Maybe a mix of urges all jumbled up like fruit in a blender. The urge to softly stroke her cheek. To tell her things would be okay, no matter how bad they seemed. To kiss her. Her cheek. Her lips. Her soul. To grab her hand. To ask her a thousand questions to probe every unseen corner of her being. To tell her she deserved better. To say that he would love her. It was crazy talk running through his head. And before he could say anything, she spoke.

"Let's go," she said.

Tom closed his laptop. He hadn't written a single word.

CHAPTER 15
PAULA

ROB SAT TYPING at his keyboard, absorbed in the mindless tedium of his work, when suddenly a strange woman in a trench coat and fedora was standing beside his desk. He jumped a little.

"Agh. Um, can I help you, ma'am?" he asked.

"You can start by cutting the 'ma'am' business. Name's Paula Daschiell." She flashed her ID. "I'm looking for the Rhodes girl. What can you tell me about her?"

"I don't know that I'm the right person to ask," said Rob.

"That's alright. You let me worry about that. Just tell me what you know."

Rob looked around for Stark like a mouse looking for a cat.

"We don't know much," Rob said. "Her last known whereabouts were at the crash. I'm sure you already know about that. We've checked with family and friends, but we've come up empty-handed. Except that we know she was troubled. We know her grades had been slipping in school, and she seemed to be experimenting with recreational drugs."

"A teen smoking pot," said Paula. "Who'd have thunk it."

"We suspect she was planning to run away with Duke Leary, who was dead on the scene."

"This is ancient history," said Paula. "Tell me something I don't know!"

"We think she was pregnant," he confided. "We found prenatal vitamins in her suitcase at the crash."

"Huh," said Paula. This was news to her. "So you think that could give us a motive? Maybe the father and Duke weren't the same person?"

"Maybe," said Rob. "Or maybe Duke was the father and someone wasn't happy about it."

"Maybe you should get the hell out of my police station and quit obstructing my investigation." It was a high, thin, and unfortunately familiar voice.

Paula turned around and sure enough, there was the corpulent chief, his pancake of a face twisted in an angry scowl.

"You sure do know how to make a dame feel special," said Paula. "You must be beating them off with a stick, going around with a line like that."

"Oh, you think you're so fucking cute," said Stark. He dropped to a snarling whisper and put his face so close to hers she could smell the garlic on his breath. "On my time, I'd belt your ass for sassing me and whoever let you out kitchen would get it twice. But I've got a fucking investigation to run, so you can leave on your own or I can have you removed. Your pick."

"Oh no!" said Paula, pantomiming fear. "I haven't inconvenienced the men, have I?" Then, seriously: "Sure, I'm leaving. I'll find this girl before you can find your tiny, shriveled-"

Stark brought the back of his hand to Paula's cheek with a loud smack. She staggered back as her hat flew off, landing a yard away. The police station fell silent, and every head turned towards Paula and the chief.

"Get out," he said through barred teeth.

Paula's eyes burned into him with rage. But she said nothing. She collected her hat off the floor, brushed off her shoulders and walked out the door with her head held high. Stark felt the eyes of the room upon him in every direction.

"Back to work!" he barked.

People returned slowly to their work, but a quiet stillness remained beneath the clacking keyboards and hushed voices. Rob looked up at the chief, but soon withered under his gaze and returned his attention to the monitor before him.

CHAPTER 16
DATH ISLAND - 1944

THE MIDDAY SUN *hung high in the summer sky, beating down hard upon the little beach town. From buildings and windows, American flags lolled in the lazy breeze. Drab green trucks bounced down the newly paved roads, bound for the tiny air force base that had been recently cobbled together on the island's southern side. A woman strolled down the street in modest heels, passing posted signs for Liberty Bonds and sun-bleached recruitment posters whose target audience had long since joined the fray. A pair of brash young men in Navy attire whistled as she passed them.*

"Get wiped," she said.

The two men turned to one another and laughed, but carried on.

She stopped and entered a building at a door with "Queen & Daschiell, Private Investigative Services" engraved on a shiny brass plaque.

"Morning, Ronnie," said the woman. She removed her fedora and set it on a hook by the door.

"Good morning, Paula," said the man behind the pine wood desk before launching into a coughing fit. What hair he had left was silver-gray. His clothes hung slack on his rail-thin body. When he'd recovered, he fished a pack of Lucky Strikes from his pocket and shook out a cigarette. "There's a new one for you today."

"What's the scoop?" she asked.

"A girl," said Ronnie, lighting his cigarette. "Dead."

"Not another one!" said Paula.

"I'm afraid so," said Ronnie. "Her brother came by this morning. Dropped off a recent photograph." Ronnie laid the photo on the desk.

Paula went over to look at the picture. The slick black and white square showed a round-cheeked girl with ribbons tying her pigtails back.

"Recent photograph?" said Paula. "Why, she can't be thirteen yet."

"Eleven," said Ronnie grimly. He took a drag on his cigarette while looking sadly into the photo. "I got the details I could from the coroner's reports. Looks like the injuries were consistent with the other two."

"Murder," said Paula. It wasn't a statement and it wasn't a question. It was a thought she rolled around her mind like a marble being rolled around in a paper cup.

"The official cause of death is an animal attack," said Ronnie. "But, given the consistency with the other two, her brother's not convinced. He's sinking his last dime into finding out what really happened."

"Alright," said Paula. "So where do we start?"

CHAPTER 17
TOM

TOM LET OUT a low whistle as the Nauti Gull came into view. She was still afloat, but the rear was covered in bent metal, deep scratches, and blue blood. Lisa and he were mounting the splintery wooden steps of the dock. The ships moored there bobbed peacefully to the splash of the water. Overhead, gulls flew and called.

Nearby on the pier, an old man was casting his fishing line into the water, playing with the line. Tom made eye contact with the old man who looked away quickly.

A young man was raising the jib on his Thistle, preparing to shove off. A parent was scolding a pair of noisy children in the parking lot. A seagull came to land on a nearby box where visitors could shove a few dollars in a slot to avoid having their car towed.

"Wow," said Tom, regarding Lisa's damaged vessel. "That must have been some crab.

"That's what I've been trying to tell everyone," said Lisa. "Only nobody believes me. I know it sounds pretty far-fetched. I'm just glad at least one person knows about it besides me."

"Once we find that claw, we'll have our proof. And we might be one step closer to finding Rhonda Rhodes." Then he added, "She's a nice boat."

"Thanks," said Lisa. "I live here."

"Wow," Tom said. "Full-time? I've never met anyone who lives on a boat, truth be told."

"I love the water," Lisa said with a shrug. Then, gesturing to the boat, she added, "After you."

Tom put one over the gunwale. No sooner had it touched the swaying deck than he realized something. "Oh!" he said. "I'd better get my laptop. I've got a report due in a couple of hours and should be taking notes. I left it in your car."

"Sure," said Lisa. "Let me just unlock it for you."

She went to the car, and Tom followed when a hot blast sent him sprawling onto the deck. A yellow-white flash blinded him as a percussive roar set his ears ringing. Wood and metal scraps fell like rain. Behind him, what was left in the boat was a ball of flame. A thick, black column of smoke rose into the air.

Tom struggled to his feet. He found Lisa crumpled against a wooden post. Blood was beginning to flow from a wound on her forehead.

"Are you alright?" he asked, helping her to her feet. He could scarcely hear himself over the shrill whining of his eardrums.

"I'm okay," she said. "My boat!!! Wha- what?- Was it a gas leak?"

"I don't think so," said Tom. "I think someone rigged it to blow just after we set foot on the boat."

"To kill us?!" said Lisa. "To kill... me? But why?!"

"Because we're getting close to the truth," said Tom. "And someone doesn't like it."

Tom looked around. Everyone in the area regarded the wreckage with shocked faces. Tom noted that the old fisherman was nowhere to be seen.

"Come on," said Tom. "Let's get out of here. Can you drive?"

"I- I don't..."

"Here, I'll drive," said Tom.

She handed him the keys as they both got into the car and slammed the door.

Tom's knees were pressed to his chest. He slid the seat back several inches, cranked it, and sped backwards. He shifted it into drive. The tires spat gravel as the Volkswagen left the parking lot and merged onto the road.

"Where are we going?" Lisa asked.

"I don't know yet," said Tom.

He adjusted the rear-view mirror so he could see out the back window. Behind them was a blue sedan, followed by a large white truck. At the next intersection, he turned right. Then left. Then two rights and another left. He drove straight for a couple of blocks. The rear-view mirror showed neither car.

Up and down the streets people passed, untroubled

by the blast that ended any sense of normality to which Tom had clung. His hands shook. He realized he'd been holding his breath and let it out. A silver-haired lady in neon pants came jogging by. A sign ahead caught Tom's eye. It promised the coldest beer in town. In the passenger seat, Lisa sat squarely facing the world beyond the windshield, her eyes a glazed blank.

The phone rang in Tom's pocket. He reached for it, dropped it between the seats, and fished it out with two fingers. "Hello," he said.

"Tom," said the voice on the other end. "Dirk here. How's that piece coming?"

"It'll be a little late," said Tom.

"Late? The hell do you mean late?"

A thousand words rose up to leap from Tom's chest. They all caught together in a tangled mess in his throat.

"Listen," Dirk continued. "What've you got from that woman PI?"

"I can't talk now, Dirk," said Tom. "I'll tell you everything as soon as I can."

"The he-"

Tom disconnected the call and tossed the phone in his lap. He pulled into a small parking lot behind an oyster bar and parked the Volkswagen. He needed time to think.

"What's happening?" said Lisa. Her eyes began to well with tears. "What the hell is happening today?"

"Something big," said Tom.

"I... I just don't... crabs, murder, the girl, my boat...

people are trying to kill me." Though tears fell, her tone was even, her voice as hollow as a pipe.

"Hey, it's going to be alright," Tom said. "We just need to keep our heads and think."

Lisa nodded.

In his mind, Tom weighed the options. They could go back home to his motel. There was no guarantee of safety there. If they rigged a bomb for Lisa, there's no telling if they might do the same for him. The Island Eye offices might be a safer bet. It was doubtful that whoever was behind this would choose to attack him in such a public place. Even so, it was a place he could be easily tracked to, and the thought gave him goose-bumps. Then his thoughts turned to Paula. It seemed the only option that made any sense.

Tom picked up the phone from his lap and fished Paula's business card from his wallet. It rang three times and went to voicemail. He swore under his breath. Then he sent a text. "Call me." He threw the phone back into his lap and rubbed his throbbing temples. The wall in front of them was painted brick. It showed cartoon oysters with large bubble eyes enjoying cutely ironic activities like fishing and snorkeling.

"Are you hungry?" Tom asked.

"Yes," she said. "I just realized I haven't eaten all day."

"Me too," said Tom. "Do you like oysters?"

"I do," she said. "But I can't go in dressed this way." Lisa was still wearing her wetsuit.

Tom looked around at the preponderance of clutter that littered the back seat.

"Do you have any clothes back here?"

"Hmm," she said. She leaned over the console into the backseat. Her rubber-clad buttocks waved about in the air. "I think I- yes! I'm going to change back here. No peeking."

Tom kept his eyes front while the car jostled around. Finally, she emerged from the rear driver's side door. A sandy beach blanket and a few balled up receipts toppled after her. She was now dressed in jeans and a wrinkled, oversized T-shirt which read "Life's a Beach." Her flip-flops were green with glitter in their plastic straps.

"How do I look?" she asked.

"Like you got dressed in clothes you found crumpled up in the back of your car."

"You're one to talk," she laughed, tussling her hair and pulling out a splintered piece of the pier.

It was true. Tom's dress shirt was slightly blackened on the back and right arm. Small holes were burned in the fabric, and one shoulder was torn. Not that it had looked great when he'd thrown it in on early this morning, but it was hardly inconspicuous.

"You don't happen to have another shirt back there, do you?" he asked.

"I think so." She rummaged through the backseat and then snickered.

"Find something?" he asked.

"I don't think you'll like it."

"Try me."

She held up a stretchy pink shirt, low cut in the neck and tightly tapered at the waist. She presented it like a prize a lucky game show contestant might stand to win.

"Hmm," said Tom. "I'll trade you."

"Aw, come on, Tom. Don't be such a wet blanket," she said. "I think you just want an excuse to get my shirt off again."

Tom let silence be his answer. She rolled her eyes.

"Turn around," she said. She climbed back into the back seat. A moment later, she handed Tom the 'Life's a Beach' shirt. It was big even for him, but somehow it made him feel a bit less like someone had tried to murder him with an incendiary bomb in the past few minutes. It smelled like dryer sheets and the jasmine perfume that pervaded the car.

Several blocks over, the shrill wailing of fire truck sirens cried urgently. It was a safe bet they were heading for the docks. Headlines danced in Tom's imagination. Somebody would report it. It was big news. It was the sort of story Tom might have rushed off to report on if he weren't so busy making it.

It struck him that he didn't know the protocol of what to do in the minutes following an attack on one's life. He realized it was a subject that now seemed conspicuously absent in all the newspaper articles he'd ever written or read. Lisa climbed out of the car and smiled at him. She looked fresh and full of life, even though they'd barely just escaped their brush with death. He smiled back.

In fact, the calmness and normalcy of the moment rang dissonantly in Tom's sense of reason. It seemed shockingly wrong that the two of them should meld so well into the unassuming flow of pedestrians as they strolled down the sun-kissed sidewalk and into the oyster bar. Like a stolen moment or the eye of a storm.

PART TWO
ACT II

CHAPTER 18
TOM

THE DOOR to the oyster bar was covered by a weather-beaten awning bearing the name of the place in cracked, peeling lettering: "Just Shucking Around."

Someone had tied little bells on a string to the doorknob inside. As Tom opened the door, they made a happy tinkling sound. He held the door for Lisa and followed her inside. He felt the laughing clams decorating the exterior might have oversold the cheeriness of the place. The interior was about the same temperature as outside. In lieu of air conditioning, fans clung to the high ceilings and turned lazy rotations as though they were paid minimum wage and keeping an eye on the clock. "Record Run" by the Beach Boys played distortedly through tinny speakers in an attempt to infuse liveliness into the sleepy restaurant, which worked about as well as the fans.

The only two patrons of the oyster bar sat on high, spindly-legged barstools. They didn't look up asTom and Lisa entered. A listless cashier in a hair net and plastic apron stood beneath a surfboard suspended from the ceiling, painted with a half dozen menu items.

"Welcome to Just Shuckin' Around, home of the bottomless oyster bucket," she droned in a dull monotone. "What can I get started for you?"

Tom placed two orders of fried oyster baskets. He glanced at a glass door refrigerator behind the counter and added two beers to the order. Tom found that his credit card was partly melted.

"I've got this one," said Lisa.

The listless cashier handed them a number to place on their table. It was number 13 and showed a pair of cartoon clams playing putt-putt golf. They took a window seat in a sticky booth along the far wall.

"Did that woman call back yet?" asked Lisa.

"Paula?" Tom said, checking his phone. "No, not yet."

"You should try her again."

Tom dialed the number. Still no answer.

"This is bad," said Lisa. "I mean, has anything like this happened to you before when you were investigating stories?"

"No," Tom said, squeezing a sliver of lime carefully into his bottle of beer. "Lately I've been covering soft pieces. Fluff really. I haven't been in the shit since LA. Even then, it was nothing like this." He lifted his bottle. "What do we drink to?"

"How about 'to being here in one piece,'" said Lisa.

"Cheers to that," said Tom. They clinked bottles, and

Tom took a long pull. The cold beer filled his mouth like the elixir of life. It rushed down his throat with merciful effervescence. Warmth spread from his belly to his limbs and brain. He felt every muscle in his body begin to relax.

The server came with a tray of steaming fried oysters and set it on the table between them. Tom nearly burnt his mouth in his eagerness to fill his belly. He hadn't realized just how hungry the day's excitement had made him. They ate in silence until the baskets were empty except for greasy wax paper and crumbs.

The phone in Tom's pocket buzzed. It was Paula.

"Paula," said Tom. "Where have you been?"

"Never mind that," she said. "What'd you find out?"

"Someone's not happy about our investigation. They blew up Lisa's boat, hoping we'd be on it," said Tom.

"Good *night*! Are you kids alright?"

"We're okay," said Tom. "But we're all out in the open here and need a place to regroup."

"My place is on the northside of town. Can you make it here without being followed?"

"I think so," said Tom. She gave him the address, which he jotted down on the back of a paper napkin.

He looked up to see someone he recognized strolling down the sidewalk out of the window just

beside him. He was short and clean-shaven, wearing dark sunshades and a bucket hat. Tom

ducked as if he'd dropped something on the floor.

"See you there," he whispered into the phone and hung up. Then to Lisa: "We've got to go."

"Why?" said Lisa.

Tom pointed out the window. "He was at the dock just before the bomb exploded and

disappeared right after it blew."

"You think he's following us?"

"I don't think he's here to hand us a get-well card."

The man rounded the corner of the block, heading for the only door to the oyster bar.

"Come on," said Tom. "We've got to move."

He took Lisa's hand and led her down the short hallway to the bathrooms. Behind them, bells jingled as the front restaurant door opened. There were three doors in the hall labeled "men's," "women's," and "employees only."

Tom opened the third door, which led into the galley kitchen with rubber non-slip pads lining the floor. Two cooks in greasy aprons looked up with wide eyes at them. A cutaway in the wall to the right was like a window without glass. It opened to the front of the restaurant just behind the cashier. Through it the man in sunshades and bucket hat was looking straight at them. He darted towards the bathroom hall.

Tom and Lisa pushed past the cooks and through the fire exit door. A tinny alarm screeched as it opened. Behind them, the man in shades burst through the door to the kitchen. Lisa pulled over a wire shelf filled with cans of sauce and big plastic jugs of oil, sending the contents toppling down, forming a barrier between them and their pursuer.

Outside was the parking lot. Lisa unlocked the

door and they both piled in. Lisa cranked the car as the man in shades clamored over the toppled shelving and out the emergency door, showing more agility and probably fewer years than his get-up made him appear.

Lisa put it in reverse and stomped on the accelerator. As she shifted into drive, the man in shades reached a hand into his windbreaker and produced a small, black pistol. The loud report cracked through the air as the rear windshield split into a thousand tiny pebbles. Aging pedestrians leapt for safety as the Volkswagen swung out onto the sidewalk before screeching onto the street.

"Fuck!" said Lisa. "Fuck fuck fuck!!!"

"Are you okay?" Tom asked.

"No, I'm not okay!" she said. "Fucking giant crabs are attacking, my fucking boat exploded, I'm fucking homeless, and now people are fucking shooting at me!!!"

"Are you shot?"

"No," she said.

"Well, that's one good thing."

"Fuck!"

Tom's own blood was thumping in his ears so loud he could hardly think.

"I think we should call a cab."

"What?" said Lisa. "Why?!"

"Because they'll probably be looking for this car."

"If we sit around waiting for a cab, we're sitting ducks. If that man could find us at the restaurant, they can find us anywhere. And I don't even know who 'they' are!"

"Okay," said Tom. He gave her the address. "But let's take the back roads and drive easy. You want to switch?"

"No," said Lisa. "I need to drive. I'll go crazy if I just sit there."

"Okay."

They turned east, passing through the old historic district. Old houses made of brick or stone were adorned with faux Roman columns made of wood. The salty air made their paint peel. The single pane glass of their windows gleamed blinding white in the sun's relentless glow. Old people rocking on their porches swiveled their heads to watch the Volkswagen passing. Driving through the monied neighborhood, the broken rear windshield felt to Tom like parading around with a glowing target on his back.

They turned north and the houses became more sparse as the road cut through the edge of the untamed jungle. Lush greenery was occasionally by driveways flanked by pretentious walls leading to ostentatious manor homes set far back from the road. In a few miles, they took a turnoff heading west, rejoining the world of the plebeians. They passed dirty convenience store gas stations with barred windows, discount oil change, pawn shops, and extended stay hotels. They turned down a narrow side street and then onto an alley. A mangy cat scurried away behind a row of overstuffed garbage bins. In the middle of the alley was a small parking area behind a two-story quadplex with window-mounted air conditioners protruding like rusting afterthoughts of comfort. They pulled into an empty space and Lisa cut the ignition. They sat for a moment in silence as though waiting for some sense of equilibrium to return.

The sun was beginning to cast long shadows, as though the world were tilting away from all that was light. For a moment, Tom was gripped with the feeling that gravity was conspiring against him. That his grip would fail and he would go tumbling off the face of the earth into the vast, lonely abyss of space. A silent scream forgotten by time.

A gentle weight on his leg roused him from his reverie, as Lisa placed her hand just above his knee. He met her eyes. They were filled with a pleading quality that plucked him out of all his cares like a honeysuckle plucked from a rambling vine. Her lips were tender and full. They melted against his like snow in an ungloved hand. The scent of her filled his senses. Her hand caressed the nape of his neck. Locks of her golden hair brushed lightly against his stubbled cheeks. When she broke the kiss, she lay her against his shoulder. He held her as she wept.

"Alright," she said. She lifted her head and sniffed. "I think I'm ready."

"Here." Tom handed her a tissue from a box found amid the things on the floorboard. "You sure? We can take a minute?"

"I'm sure."

A wind was beginning to blow. Distant clouds were gathering far off in the eastern skies.

They exited the car and passed through a creaking wrought iron gate. A rusty stairwell led upwards, moaning under each step. On the landing, a potted plant hung limply from a hook. Tom rapped his knuckles on the hollow-core door.

CHAPTER 19
PAULA: EARLIER THAT DAY

PAULA RUBBED her glove hand against her cheek. It still stung from the back of Chief Stark's meaty hand. A rage was boiling inside her. A lust for revenge. She shrugged off these thoughts. They were dangerous thoughts with the full moon so near.

The police station now was a diminishing speck in the Stingray's rear-view mirror. With the next turn, it was out of her sight completely.

She drove north, taking the scenic coastal route. The car's top was down, and the sound of the surf crashing against the sand was soothing. She inhaled deep lung-fuls of the briny air. Some children played and screamed on the beach. Seniors lounged on plastic chairs, fried like bacon in the sun.

The road turned inland. Palm trees and verdant undergrowth blocked the ocean from view. The road climbed gently and wound its way farther and farther from town. Few cars passed in the opposite direction, and none seemed to be heading north with Paula.

After several miles, Paula turned off down a gravel road which climbed still higher as it cut its way through the dense foliage. The road was adorned sparsely with mailboxes for houses, many of which were set too far back from the road to be seen. One such "mailbox" was constructed out of an old microwave. It had been lashed to a post and had the street number scrawled on the side in red paint. Paula turned onto this drive and stopped at a sagging utility gate. Beside this gate was an intercom system consisting of a Walkie Talkie shielded from the elements by a three-sided box made of old license plates.

Paula pressed the button on the Walkie Talkie.

"Hello? Emilio?" she said.

For a moment, there was silence.

"Emilio?" she tried again.

"Who is it and what do you want?" a voice crackled through the speaker.

"It's Paula," she said. "I need your help."

"-second," the walkie-talkie said.

Paula put her fists in her trench coat pockets. She kicked a pebble with her toe and looked up and down the empty road. After a time, she heard a whirring sound behind her. Beyond the utility gate, a squat little man in a golf cart was making his way down the drive.

The man had round, bottle glasses that magnified his eyes to an alarming size. His gray hair was pulled back into a ponytail that came down to his belt line. Gray hairs protruded from his ears and nostrils and a tobacco-stained goatee encircled his pink mouth. A tie-dyed shirt stretched across this gut. And pale legs protruded from his cargo shorts, terminating in close-toed sandals worn with socks.

He dismounted the golf cart and sidled over to unlock the gate.

"How are you, Emilio?" asked Paula. "I tried to call ahead. You didn't answer."

"Don't use the cell phone anymore," Emilio shook his head. His ponytail waved. "The new towers. They hijack the mental waves."

"What about the land line?"

Emilio shook his head. "Damn utility companies," he said simply. He locked the gate behind them.

They got into the golf cart and turned around. As they bounced their way up the drive towards the house, warning signs passed like billboards for an upcoming roadside attraction: "No trespassing," "Keep out," "Trespassers will be shot. Survivors will be shot again. Beware attack dog," and the like.

The house came into view. It might well have been described as a shack. A single wide trailer had been doubled in size by the addition of corrugated metal sheets and upcycled windows of various sizes. A blue plastic tarp hung over a section of the roof beneath a large array of solar panels. The porch was made of old wooden pallets and boasted a shabby couch covered in Mexican blankets.

The golf cart pulled to a stop in front of the dilapidated house. Paula followed Emilio as he shuffled up to the front steps and pulled open the door. A blue heeler burst through the door and began jumping up with his paws on Emilio's chest.

"Down! *Get* down!" he said. The dog growled and raised its hackles when it spotted Paula. "Cut that out." Emilio grabbed the dog by the collar. "Excuse Pedro. He's friendly, just excited. Sit!"

Pedro had stopped barking. He sat breathing hard, watching Paula intently as she climbed the cinder block steps into the trailer.

The interior of the trailer was hot and dim. The sink was piled with dishes and dirty trails on the shag carpet made paths that all seemed to radiate from the couch. A huge section of the wall had been removed, leading to the extension.

"You want a beer?" Emilio asked. He shut the door behind him.

"No thanks," said Paula. "I'm working."

Emilio shrugged. He shuffled to the fridge and grabbed a tall can of Natural Ice. He pulled a hand-rolled cigarette from behind his ear and fired it up.

"You say you need help?" he asked, the cigarette wagging between his lips.

"I found something," said Paula. "I don't know what it is, but I'm hoping you can tell me. It could be important."

She produced the round device with the blinking red light and metal teeth. Emilio took it between two fingers and frowned at it.

"Ever seen anything like it before?"

"No," said Emilio. "Let's have a look at it in the light."

He flipped a switch, and the corrugated metal extension lit up with strings of multicolored Christmas lights. The room might have been the lab of a redneck mad scientist. Ancient computer monitors were strapped together, forming a wall of screens. The pegboard lining the walls was covered in tools and the perimeter was all workbenches. The half-assembled devices upon them looked as though they might have been recovered from an alien craft.

Emilio grunted as he hoisted himself onto a barstool. He flipped on a halogen lamp and grabbed a jeweler's lens off the workbench. He picked up the mysterious device with a pair of needle-nosed pliers. He squinted at it through the lens.

"Hmm," he said. "No, I never have. Looks factory-made. Where'd you find it?"

"In the mountains by a crashed car," she said. "A girl went missing there. I'm hoping maybe this can help me find her. Or at least point me in the right direction."

"Huh," said Emilio. "This isn't any kind of car part I've ever seen. Look at these teeth on the bottom. Looks like it was supposed to hook into something. It's well constructed, but you can see a little seam here if you hold it up to the light. We might be able to pop it open. Do you mind?"

"Go right ahead."

Emilio took a flat-head screwdriver sharpened to a

fine edge and pried the black plastic of the housing apart. Inside was a small silicone board packed with chips and transistors.

"Interesting," he said. "It's waterproof. You see this rubber gasket here? And this housing is really sturdy stuff. Looks like bulletproof plastic."

"What does it do?" Paula asked.

"Hold on." Emilio flipped a switch, and the wall of monitors came to life. "Funny. It looks an awful lot like parts you'd find in a cell phone." He waved a wand that looked suspiciously like a curling iron over the device in his hand.

"Yep. It's sending and receiving signals of some kind."

"Can you trace where it's coming from?"

"Maybe. It'd take some time." Emilio took a deep drag from his cigarette and a hit of his beer. "I don't know. I don't like having this kind of stuff around. It gives me the creeps."

"I'm asking for your help," said Paula. "A girl's missing. Maybe she's dead, but maybe she's not. Right now, this is the best lead I've got."

Emilio stared at the gutted transmitter before him. He took a few more puffs.

"Alright," he said at last. "Come back in a couple hours."

"You're the best," Paula said. She planted a kiss on the top of his greasy head of hair.

His glasses nearly fell off his nose.

She turned to leave.

"Oh, wait," said Emilio. "Let me get that damn dog."

He drove Paula back to the gate.

She told him she'd see him in a couple of hours and climbed back into the Stingray. The wind was beginning to blow and clouds gathered in the eastern sky. But the verdant woods were still drenched in warm sunlight and the breeze was pleasant on Paula's face.

She scanned the radio and found a station playing classical music. Brahms, perhaps? She was halfway to the paved road when her cell phone rang. The display showed it was Tom. She answered.

"Where have you been?" said Tom.

He proceeded to tell her that a bomb had been placed on Lisa's boat. It was meant to kill them. And that someone had been sent after them to finish the job.

She gave him the address to her place and told him to meet her there.

She sped home and parked the Stingray behind the apartment. She left it uncovered and climbed the steps to the second-story flat. She undid the two deadbolts that secured the door. And stepped inside the modest room. No sooner had she entered when someone from behind the door threw an arm around her neck. She dropped her weight and tried to turn, throwing an elbow which missed her mark as the attacker stepped back. Powerful arms threw her on the bed. The mattress squeaked as she turned to see a dark woman with deep hazel eyes straddling her from above. The woman held Paula's wrists above her head and planted a soft kiss on her lips.

"Hey, baby," she said.

"Jesus, Kelly! You want to give me apoplexy? Let me up."

"I just wanted to have a little fun before the full moon. That's all. You're not in the mood, huh?"

"It's not that," Paula said. "I'm working. There's a girl missing."

"The Rhodes girl?"

"That's the one."

"I read about it in the paper. You got any leads?"

"Maybe. We're on to someone who doesn't like us getting so close to the truth. The reporter on the beat and the girl who saw something are getting shot at. Incidentally, they're on their way here."

"Wait, what?"

There was a knock on the door. Kelly grabbed a revolver from the nightstand drawer and went to answer it.

CHAPTER 20
TOM

THERE WAS the sound of footsteps nearing the door, and someone asked, "Who is it?" The voice was as unfamiliar as it was unfriendly.

"Tom and Lisa," Tom said.

There was the scratch and click of several chains and locks being disengaged. When the door peaked open, the first thing to appear was the glinting steel of a fat, six shot revolver leveled squarely at Tom's chest. The gun was held by a five and a half foot woman with beautifully dark skin and an expression on her face that could curdle milk. She wore a tight black halter top and a neatly spherical Afro like a dark halo. Her pants were sand colored bell-bottoms. But mostly, Tom kept his eye on the gun.

"Easy, Kelly," came a voice from somewhere inside. "That's them."

She lowered the gun and stepped aside.

Paula sat up in the bed, tying the sash around her trench coat.

"Tom. Lisa. This is Kelly," said Paula. "Kelly, Tom and Lisa."

"Nice to meet you," said Tom, extending a hand.

"Well, it's a liability to meet you," Kelly replied.

"Take it easy, babe," said Paula.

"Do you really expect me to be happy you're inviting over strangers being trailed by hitmen? They're probably going to lead them right to this apartment."

"Hey," said Lisa. "I didn't ask for any of this. And we wouldn't have come if we weren't invited."

"It doesn't matter what you asked for or didn't-"

"-I was shot at!"

"-leading them back to my house-"

"-goddammit-"

Paula put her fingers in her mouth and loosed a high-pitched whistle. The room got quiet and everyone looked her way.

"Cool it," Paula said. She raised a hand like a witness swearing in. "Now, let's all try this again. Kelly, these are friends of mine and they're in a bind- let me finish. I'm up to my neck in this as much as they are. And Lisa's right, I did invite them. So if you're blaming anyone, you can blame me. Tom, Lisa, you're pretty hot right now. The way things are, it's pretty understandable why someone wouldn't be happy to see you, so I hope you don't take it personally. Now, however it happened, we're all together, so can we all shake hands and be nice. Even if it's just a personal favor to me."

Kelly's arms were folded. She was looking at Paula with hard eyes.

"You know you kill me, Paula," said Kelly. "You really kill me."

"Love you, babe," Paula winked.

Kelly sighed and unfolded her arms.

"Fine," Kelly said. "I don't like it, but fine." She turned to Tom and Lisa. "I'm Kelly."

She shook hands with them both.

"Kelly teaches self-defense lessons downtown," said Paula. "She's got a couple black belts, so try to stay on her good side." Then to Kelly, "Tom writes for the Eye and Lisa's a scuba instructor."

For the first time since they'd stepped inside, Tom was able to get a look around the room in which they stood.

The apartment was modest in size and cheaply furnished. It's one room served as its kitchen, bedroom, and living room all in one. Gaudy yellowed wallpaper with pink flowers peeled back from the plaster walls. There was a small bed with a metal frame and a set of handcuffs latched to one of the bars. Most of the photographs hanging from the wall or standing in frames were black and white. There was an old tube radio the size of a small refrigerator and an old manual typewriter sat on a cheap card table alongside a stack of loose-leaf copy paper. A few medals and awards hung on the wall nearest the bed. Below them was a severe-looking sword with a red tassel dangling from the pommel. Tom presumed this to belong to

Kelly. The whole room could be crossed in about six steps.

"What's the plan?" Tom asked.

Paula had crossed the room and opened a small safe. From it she produced a Glock 19 and two cardboard boxes of ammunition. She sat on the bed, feeding bullets into the magazine.

"The plan is we stay together," she said. "We're on the right track to find Rhonda or nobody would care enough to make all this fuss about stopping us. Odds are good it's only getting hotter. You packing, cowboy?" she asked Tom.

"Yeah," said Tom, feeling the comforting weight of the semi-auto in his ankle holster.

Paula snapped the loaded magazine into the Glock and handed it to Lisa.

"No thanks," said Lisa. "I hate guns."

"You hate it more than picking your brain up in chunks from off the beach?" Paula said. "Come on, you might need it."

Lisa shuddered and took the gun, tucking it into the waist of her jeans.

"I dropped something off with an old friend of mine just before you called. He's a real whiz kid. I think it could be our next big break." Paula opened the cylinder of her own revolver and inspected it. "I think he might be ready for us to pay him a visit. I say we make a field trip of it."

"Do you really think you'll need that?" Lisa asked Kelly as she took the sword down from the wall.

"This sword has helped me out of a lot of scrapes down through the years. But it never did anyone a lick of good collecting dust on this wall," said Kelly.

"This guy lives way out in the woods on the north side," said Paula. She snapped the cylinder of the revolver shut and tucked it away in a shoulder holster beneath her coat. "Your Volks is hot right now, Cousteau. Let's take the Stingray."

The wind was blowing harder now. It tugged at the door as they exited the small apartment and made their way out on the landing. Kelly locked both deadbolts. They descended the stairs and went out to the parking lot. Paula kept the Stingray under a cover. They transferred this cover to the Volkswagen. It fit poorly and needed to be weighed down with rocks to prevent it from blowing away, but it did its job in camouflaging the vehicle.

Tom and Lisa piled in the rear seat. Kelly rode shotgun. Paula brought the purring motor to life and eased the car down the alley and out onto the road. Overhead, the clouds were gathering fast.

CHAPTER 21
BRACHYURA

THE MAN in sunglasses and bucket hat stepped into the elevator. He put a key into the slot and turned it, allowing him access to the lower floors. The steel doors hissed shut and the elevator began to descend. A display showed he had dropped five stories below ground level before the doors once again opened. Here, a long hallway was cut into the rock. I was about 10 feet high and just as wide. The walls were left rough-hewn like a natural cave. The floor was porcelain tile and stainless steel handrails protruded from the rocky walls on either side of the hallway. Walking down this hall gave the man the impression of being fired from a cannon in slow motion. He shook the thought from his head and reached the double doors at the end of the hall.

These opened to a large room. The stone ceiling vaulted high overhead. The opposite wall was an enormous window set into the rock. It framed a breathtaking view of the crashing sea. Before this window was a simple desk. And behind this desk stood Dr. Brachyura.

He had his back to the man in the bucket hat. He was facing out the window as if meditating on the ocean's waves.

"What is your news?" said Brachyura without turning.

"It is unfortunate news, Sir," said the man.

Brachyura pinched the bridge of his nose and made a pained expression, yet his voice was cool and even. "Speak," said Brachyura.

"The bomb was unsuccessful, Sir. The reporter and the mark were not aboard when it ignited. I set the detonator as soon as they came aboard, but they unexpectedly deboarded just before the explosion."

Brachyura sighed.

"Is there more?" Brachyura asked.

"Yes, Sir. I was able to track them down. In a restaurant downtown."

"And yet you didn't kill them?"

"They escaped, Sir. I attempted to pursue but they fled. They were in a red Volkswagen Beetle. It now has a bullet hole in the rear windshield."

"You shot at them?" asked Brachyura.

"Yes, Sir. Whether either of them was hit, I can't say."

"And how many witnesses were there?" asked Brachyura.

"I cannot say, Sir. Perhaps ten."

"Ten," said Brachyura. He turned to face the man. "Ten people saw you attempt to kill these two."

"Yes, Sir." The man hung his head.

Brachyura regarded him in silence for a long moment.

"Let me explain something to you, Mandrake," said Brachyura. He walked around his desk and put an arm over the man's shoulder. "Come with me."

They walked towards a door in the east Wall.

"Twenty years ago, Mandrake. Twenty long years ago, I established Brachyura Industries. I had nothing but a PHD and a dream. I didn't work for anyone else, because I didn't want to do what anyone else was doing. Are you following, Mandrake? I had an original idea. And do you know what happened, Mandrake? I was mocked. I was ridiculed. Laughed at in the scientific community. Do you know the old adage about how geniuses are never truly appreciated in their own time?

"Now I make no claim to genius, Mandrake. Far from it. I was merely given a seed of inspiration many years ago. And I nurtured it. I watered it. I cared for it. I let no one dissuade me from it. It was an investment of life energy. My life. Time. The one commodity given to us all that can never be replaced. Funny to think of it like that, isn't it?"

Brachyura pushed open the doors. They were in an antiseptic laboratory room now. The walls were lined with beakers and flasks. White plastic coveralls and respirators hung neatly from hooks on the walls and monitors displayed data and charts. The two men continued walking through this room towards another door on the opposite wall.

"I remember all my boyhood, Mandrake. I remember all the men I admired. Roosevelt. Churchill. Washington. Now, Washington's an interesting one. He was the only US president to ever win unanimously. Did you know that, Mandrake? And that touches on my point. The unifying thread of all the men that I admired, many more than I have mentioned here, is that they had influence. There's an interesting word, isn't there? It means the ability to make others do what *you* want them to. Can you think of anything more worthy of pursuing? Of course not! There isn't one. I put it to you, Mandrake. Give me one cause- and you needn't bother now, this is just for rhetoric's sake- one cause worthy of pursuing and I say to you that it means nothing if you cannot *influence* others to also pursue it."

They now reached the door on the far end of the lab. This door led to a much larger room spanning two stories. As they pushed through the door, they found themselves on a catwalk that ran around the circumference of the room and cut a path through it. Below were at least a dozen round tanks of water. They were open at the top and so near the catwalk that one could easily bend down and dip a finger into the water.

"It sounds like a vague concept," Brachyura continued, "doesn't it? One can't very well take influence, put it in a box, slap a price label on it and ship it out the door, can one, Mandrake? And yet, that was my idea. Look here."

Brachyura flipped a switch on the wall. The tanks filled with light and Mandrake could suddenly see they were each filled with something enormous that moved and scuttled in the water.

"Is- Are those-?" Mandrake began.

"Crabs?" said Brachyura. "Yes. They've mutated of course. It was never my intention to create them. Just a funny byproduct of dumping some waste materials from my main project into the sea. BUT! I came to realize, as I perfected my primary invention, that they were a great boon to me. My *primary* invention is this."

Brachyura held up a small, round device with a blinking red light.

"What is it, Sir?" asked Mandrake.

"This, Mandrake, is pure influence. The Mind Ray. You see those crabs? Each of them has one of these attached to their heads. You see tank number two? That one there. He will snap his right claw...now."

Brachyura pulled a remote from his breast and pressed a button. Obediently, the mutant crab snapped his right claw.

"Oh my! This is most impressive, Sir!" said Mandrake.

"It's nothing, Mandrake. Nothing compared to what it shall be when it is complete. When it's complete, this device will be small enough to fit inside almost anything. And it won't require contact. It will be able to transmit its signal using proximity. This renders anyone and everyone subject to the will of whoever controls it. And everyone will carry one with them. All day. Every day. Everywhere they go."

"How is that, Sir?"

Brachyura's eyes beamed with delight.

"What do you have in your pockets right now, Mandrake?"

"Uh... keys, a wallet, a phone..."

"A phone," said Brachyura. He held the blinking device before him. "This will be small enough to fit inside any and every phone, leaving every production factory in the world. That phone's owner will be subject to anything they are told to do. To buy a certain service. A certain product. To vote a certain way. To work more. To complain less. In essence, this," he held up the device, "is everything I've given my life to. And it will soon be realized."

Brachyura led Mandrake to the edge of the railing, peering over the giant crabs.

"Soon. Very soon, Mandrake, I will be in negotiations with governments and industries to lease this technology to the highest bidder. I will be the wealthiest man in the world by unfathomable orders of magnitude. That is," he said, lowering his tone, "provided some brain-dead fool doesn't muck it up."

With a sudden push, Brachyura pushed Mandrake over the railing, sending him splashing into the water. Mandrake bobbed to the surface of the water. Shock and terror widened his eyes.

"These crabs will do more than any hired goon," said Brachyura.

"No! Wait!" Mandrake pleaded.

"So long," said Brachyura. He pressed a button on his remote.

The crab sprang to life. Spread its mottled claws above its head, catching Mandrake's torso between its pincers.

"NOOOOOOOOOoooooooOOOOOOOOooooooo-OOOOO!!!!!!!!!" Mandrake screamed as the claws ripped him in half. It flailed his body like a rag doll, churning the water red.

Brachyura turned his back on the tanks and left the crab to feed.

"It's so hard finding good help these days," he said.

He walked back to the room with the monitors. He pulled up the display, which showed the location of the tracking device that had gone missing. He knew that it was no longer attached to any crab. That would not be possible given the great distance it had covered inland. If that had happened, there would have been a deluge of reports from frightened citizens. In all probability, that girl had it. The one who came into the police station in scuba gear, screaming about how she'd seen a crab.

"Well," Brachyura said to himself. "Let's try this one more time. If we can't trust a hit man, then perhaps we can trust the Mind Ray." He looked back to the door nearest the catwalk. "Oh, I suppose I could send the two or three of them that haven't eaten yet today."

He looked back to a room he had not shown the late

Mandrake. A room that contained the young woman. There could be many uses for the Mind Ray, Brachyura mused. But that would have to be his side project. For the time being, the primary objective was- the scuba instructor girl must die.

CHAPTER 22

TOM

PAULA DROVE CAREFULLY, coming to a full stop at each red light and signaling every turn. She glanced back at the rear-view mirror often.

The passengers all gazed out the windows as if in deep meditation. Overhead, the clouds were beginning to crowd out all the blue from the sky. They made shadows as they passed under the sun, so the daylight had a dappled quality like a desk lamp as seen from the bottom of a fish tank. Tom checked his phone. He'd missed seven calls from Dirk Daily at the Island Eye. A primal part of him panicked, some vestige from the hunter-gatherer instinct, dreading the disastrous loss of a food source. This impulse was quickly dispelled by the realization that this story would be the biggest of his life if he lived long enough to tell it. This thought was replaced with shame at that selfishness when he thought of Rhonda Rhodes, whose chances of being found alive were diminishing with each passing moment.

Tom drummed his fingers on the window ledge for a moment. The silence was becoming insufferable, and he decided to end it.

"So, Kelly," said Tom. "What's your story? Are you from around here?"

"What, are we at summer camp now?" Kelly said. "Getting to know each other?"

"No, I guess not," said Tom.

"Look," said Kelly. She turned around in her seat so she was facing Tom. "You brought trouble to my door. You came into my life. And you know what? Fine. Paula makes a career out of sniffing out trouble and maybe I've got to accept that once in a while some dirt's going to blow in through the front door when she comes home. But me? I've had enough trouble to last ten life-times with some left over. So let me make something clear. I'm here for two reasons and two reasons only. Number one: That Rhodes girl is missing, right? So we're gonna find her. I don't like to see a young girl in trouble. And number two: As much as I don't like it, sitting in this car now seems a lot smarter than sitting at home waiting for the next knock on the door, which might be from somebody who's not delivering pizza."

"She's a real laugh at parties too," said Paula.

"Don't do that," said Kelly. "Don't minimize this. We are in some serious shit right now."

"I can't believe they blew up my boat," said Lisa.

She might have been talking to herself. She was gazing absently through the glass at the scenery passing by. Kelly looked over at her for a moment.

"Hey, how'd you get mixed up in this?" Kelly asked. "The reporter and Dick Tracy here, I understand. But you're a scuba instructor."

"Yeah," said Lisa. "At least I was. I was diving earlier today and I saw something. A crab bigger than my car. It attacked me. But when I went to report it to the police, nobody would listen. Then my boat blows up and now people are shooting at me."

Kelly regarded her with sympathy. Some of the tension in her jaw began to soften.

"That's heavy," she said.

"Yeah," said Lisa.

"Full moon, too," said Kelly.

"You don't believe in that superstitious stuff, do you?" asked Tom.

"Yeah," said Kelly. "Yeah, I do."

"Hey, buckle up, kids," said Paula. "We've got company."

Police lights began to flash behind them. The siren blipped a couple times for them to pull over.

"What's the speed limit here?" asked Tom.

"45," said Paula.

"How fast were we going?"

"40."

"Shit," said Kelly.

"Maybe they can help us," said Lisa.

"Sister, if you believe that, I've got some time shares to sell you," said Paula. "Just play it cool and let me do the talking. And make sure your piece isn't showing."

They were on a semi-rural stretch of road. It wasn't

too far from town, but the houses were spread out about a quarter mile apart to the left. To the right was nothing but dunes with shocks of pampas grass. Under other circumstances, it might have made for a peaceful drive. Paula turned on her blinker and eased the car onto the shoulder.

Two uniformed officers stepped out of the police car. Their chests were puffed out with bulletproof vests. They walked around to opposite sides of the Stingray. The car top was up and Paula waited until the driver's side officer rapped his knuckle on the glass before she rolled down the hand crank window.

"What seems to be the trouble, officer?"

"You ran a stop sign," said the officer. "About a half mile back."

"I don't recall any stop sign, officer. We've been heading straight northbound for the last three miles."

The other officer peered in the passenger side windows. He held a flat hand above his eyes to shield the glare.

"Happens all the time," said the driver's side officer. "These scenic roads, people get to looking around and let their minds wander. Next thing they know, they run right through a stop sign. I'm going to have to ask you to step out of the car."

"You're not going to write me a ticket?"

"Don't play it the hard way, lady. Step out of the vehicle."

"You know," said Paula. "This car might be hot. I might've stolen it this morning for all you know, because you never did ask for my license and registration."

The officer on the passenger side put a hand on the butt of his gun.

"Of course, you boys might be new, seeing as you don't have any name tags like every other cop on this island. Maybe they haven't printed them up for you yet."

After that, it all happened fast.

The passenger side officer drew his gun from his holster.

Kelly opened the latch to the passenger side door and kicked it hard into him.

He went sprawling to the ground. Paula threw the Stingray into gear and mashed the pedal to the floor. Tiny rocks went flying off like birdshot from behind the wheels.

The other officer had his gun in his hand and snapped off a bullet, which ricocheted off the hood.

The Stingray found traction on the asphalt and picked up speed.

Tom looked back and saw both officers on their feet and heading back into the squad car.

"They're not cops?" asked Lisa.

"Those goons are as phony as a three-dollar bill," said Paula. "I've seen better costumes at a Halloween party."

"Those guns are pretty damn real," said Kelly.

"Ours are too," said Paula.

Two more rounds whistled overhead. Tom looked

back and saw that one of the men was leaning out of the window, taking aim at the car. They were gaining ground fast.

"If they get much closer, those shots are going to start hitting something."

"Shoot for the tires," said Paula. She ducked as another gunshot rang out. There was a pop of metal as it pierced the car. Lisa screamed.

"Lisa!" cried Tom.

She was grasping her leg. A red patch of blood was spreading across the blue denim.

"He shot me! HE FUCKING SHOT ME!" Lisa screamed.

"Put pressure on it!" said Tom. More gunshots cracked around them.

"Quick, Tom!" said Kelly. "He's reloading."

Kelly had her window down and was already popping off rounds at the car behind. It was now only five or six car lengths away. Tom unholstered his gun and opened the back passenger door. The gun felt heavy in his hand and swayed wildly with the jostling movement of the car. He put the rear tire between the iron sights and squeezed. Again. And again. And again.

The tire rubber tore loose and flapped around the wheel like an old piece of plastic. Sparks flew as the metal rim skidded on the rough tarmacadam. The police car fishtailed slightly and began to fall behind. The cosplaying officer emerged from the window again and let off three more rounds before the car shrank into the distance and disappeared behind the tall grasses of the next bend.

"Shit!" Lisa said. She was grasping the damp crimson of her pant leg.

"How's it look, Kel?" asked Paula.

"Let me see it, baby," said Kelly.

"No no no no no," Lisa pleaded.

"It's alright. I just need to see it for a second. Just a peek."

"MMMMM," Lisa said as she removed her hand from the wound.

Kelly ripped the pant leg back to expose the wound. It was a gash about three inches long across Lisa's middle thigh. Blood began to pool in the white and pink trench it formed. Kelly grabbed a stack of napkins from the console and pressed them against the wound. Lisa choked back a yelp.

"Hold these here," Kelly said. "You're gonna be alright. I know it hurts like hell, but it just grazed you. You're gonna be alright."

Tom sucked air through his teeth.

"This is insane," he said. "I could believe this if we were taking down an arm of the cartel, but this is a high school girl we're tracking down."

"You're right," said Paula. "This isn't your run-of-the-mill kidnapping. This is someone with serious connections to pull strings on this kind of muscle."

"And we're stepping right on their toes," said Kelly.

"What, you want me to turn around and go back

there? Tell those meat necks we're real sorry about what happened, keep the girl, and no hard feelings?"

"I didn't say that," said Kelly. "I know we passed the point of no return a long way back. Probably before I even knew it happened. I'm in this with you. All the way."

Lisa groaned.

Tom put an arm around her and she leaned on his shoulder.

"It's alright," he told her.

"The guy we're going to see will take good care of that," Paula called back to Lisa. "He's got medical supplies. He's stocked up like a fallout shelter for World War III. We'll have you patched up in no time flat."

They reached the turnoff for the unpaved road, then the microwave mailbox, and finally were at Emilio's utility gate.

Paula called on the walkie-talkie and in minutes Emilio was riding his golf car like a hick chariot up to the gate.

CHAPTER 23
FAKE COPS

"SHIT!" said one of the spurious police officers. He kicked the flat tire with his steel-toed boot. "*He* is gonna hit the goddam roof!"

"For fuck's sake, Greg! You think I don't know that?!" said the other.

"This one's on you, dick wheat. 'License and registration.' That's basic shit, man!"

"How could I know that bitch would run? Besides, I didn't see you doing a goddamn thing 'cept trip over your own shoe laces and bust your ass in the tall weeds."

"Me?! I didn't even have a chance before you turned this whole fuckin' thing into a goddam soup sandwich."

"Look," the other man said. He took a deep breath. "We're here now. And somebody's got to call him. Let's flip a coin."

"Flip a fuckin' toaster on with your limp dick in it! I'm changing the spare. You make your own goddam phone call." Greg turned his back and walked off to the trunk.

"Christ on the cross," said the other man to himself. "Alright. Shit happens. Could've happened to anybody. Just call him."

He pulled up Brachyura's contact on his phone screen. He stared at it for a minute. Jiggled the phone in his hand. Then he quickly pressed the button. He closed his eyes and pulled on his earlobe as he waited for the call to connect.

"Is it done?" Brachyura's voice asked immediately as the call connected.

"Well, sir..." he began.

"Is. It. Done?" asked Brachyura.

"There were, uh... a few complications. She wasn't alone. There were two other women and a man with her. Seems they're all armed. They started shooting and managed to disable our vehicle. We, uh... we lost visual contact, sir."

There was a long silence. For a moment, the man thought the call might have dropped.

"Sir?"

"Return here at once," Brachyura said. The call ended.

"What'd he say?" asked Greg. He was positioning the jack under the car.

"He just said to get back there right away," said the man.

"We are so fucked, Cletus."

"You see that right there's the problem, Greg. You're

always thinking in the negative. Positive thoughts create positive outcomes."

"Clete," said Greg. He stood up, dropping the tire iron on the road. "You are dumber than a football bat. You fix your own goddam tire."

CHAPTER 24
BRACHYURA

ALL THE EQUIPMENT on the desk jumped and settled with a glassy clink when Brachyura slammed his fist on the tabletop. A vein shaped like a lightning bolt throbbed on his temple. His sharp eyes glinted with rage. He looked around the room. He wanted to destroy something. Or someone.

He turned his attention to the girl strapped to the table behind the glass door in the corner of the room. He lunged like a wild beast pouncing on its prey. He yanked the door open, and it slammed against the wall. The girl was still passed out from the sedatives.

"You bitch! Wake up!" Brachyura screamed. He grabbed her shoulders and shook her violently. The manacles that bound her to the bed rattled, but her face remained as impassive as a china doll's. He raised a flat hand and brought it hard against one cheek and then the other. The loud smacking sounds rang like gunshots in the tiny room. Her cheekbones hurt his knuckles. Her head tossed side to side. Droplets of blood flew from her slack lips. But she did not rouse. She was pumped with enough sedatives to tranquilize a Shetland pony. Brachyura saw that even if he started whittling her fingertips into points with a pencil sharpener, she would not stir. He kicked the table in disgust.

He realized he was behaving foolishly, like an angry child. He checked himself, smoothing into place the locks that had fallen loose from his slicked-back hair. Taking it out on the girl was not helping his situation. It was merely a distraction. He shut the glass door quietly, practicing his self-control. He was so close to the accomplishment of his goal- his life's work. This was no time for histrionics.

Twice now, he had tried without success to terminate the scuba girl with hired help. And twice they had failed him. It was clear now there was no other choice. He would have to send the crabs. Perhaps they were largely untested in this capacity, but they had been able to capture the Rhodes girl and kill that boy she was with without any trouble.

The fact that one had lost its transmitter and gone rogue was upsetting. But it was still a safer bet than sending more hapless goons who were liable to trip on their own shoelaces on the way over. That bowling ball of a police chief might be able to be bought with hush money, but Brachyura wouldn't trust him with much more than keeping quiet and passing on the odd tip. No, it seemed the crabs were his best option.

He pulled up the map on his monitor once more. The red dot seemed to have stopped moving. It was in a heavily wooded part of the jungle not too far away at the base of the mountain. That, at least, was in his favor.

The fact that the scuba girl seemed to have help- and that help had guns- was concerning, too. He would send three crabs to do the job. Perhaps it was overkill, but at this stage, he'd rather be safe than sorry.

Brachyura crossed the lab and passed through the door up onto the catwalk. He flipped a series of switches. Red lights began blinking. The room was painted in their strobing, crimson glow. A low, crooning alarm sounded. Three of the cylindrical tanks below began to empty of water. The mottled carapaces and of the crabs began to surface, and the air filled with the aquarium smell of briny water and fish. The crabs stood at attention as the cylindrical walls of their tanks spun, revealing doorways leading out to the laboratory floor below. With the pull of a lever on the wall, a set of huge blast doors on the north wall yawned open like a mechanical mouth ready to feed.

Brachyura then pulled the remote from his jacket and input a series of commands.

"Now," he said. "Find the girl and her friends. Rip them limb from limb. Eat every last shred of their flesh. Leave nothing behind."

He pressed a final button and the three crabs sprang to life like wind-up dolls. Their pointed talons clanked like the hooves of a dozen horses on the metal grate floor. With startling rapidity, their hulking forms disappeared from view down the cavernous hall, and the blast doors hissed shut behind them.

"There," he said. "Let's see you wriggle your way out of this one."

CHAPTER 25
PAULA 1944

THE OLIVE DRAB *military jeep that climbed the sun-drenched mountain was sparse and utilitarian. Its hard, angular form was barely softened by the rigid bench seat. There were no doors and no roof. As it leapt and bounded up the rocky unpaved road, Paula had the sensation more than once that she would be pitched sideways out of the vehicle and smash her head open on a rock. In spite of this, she attempted to appear stoic.*

Behind the wheel was a square-jawed youth in his mid to late twenties. He wore crisply pressed green pants, a matching jacket with an Air Force patch stitched to the shoulder, and a few decorations besides. His hat sat at a jaunty angle upon his short-cropped blond head of hair. His face bore the look of bland determination one often sees upon those waiting in line at a post office.

On a nearby branch, a long-limbed monkey scampered through the trees away from the roaring metal beast.

"So tell me," the driver asked. "What's a pretty young girl

like you doing thumbing rides to the middle of the jungle all
by your lonesome?"

Paula shot him a venomous glance, but the driver kept his
eyes on the road ahead and missed it.

"I'm on a job," she said. "A little girl got ripped apart in
the jungle. The death certificate says it was an animal. The
brother doesn't buy it."

"Why not?" asked the driver.

"For one," said Paula, "he doesn't think she walked to the
spot she was found at. Thinks she was dragged there from
near her home, which was two miles away. You know any
animal that does something like that?"

"Can't say I do," said the driver.

"Secondly," she continued, "this is the third case in the
last four months like it. All were found in roughly the same
spot. Same kind of injuries. One was a little boy, ten years old.
The other was a little girl, age 13. And thirdly, it happened on
a full moon. Just like the other two. There's a definite pattern,
only everyone's too focused on the war to connect the dots."

"You know," said the driver, "you had me going until that
full moon stuff. What do you mean by that old native super-
stition? You think a werewolf had something to do with it?"

"I'm just giving you the facts. You tell me what you make
of it."

"Sure, it's awfully sad about those kids. But this is a wild
jungle out here. Who knows what kind of animals are out
there?"

"Maybe," said Paula. "Only I've got a hunch there's
something more to it."

"Just what do you plan to do with this hunch of yours?"

"I'm going to interview the tribes. Something nobody bothered to do yet."

"I've gotta tell ya," said the driver, "I feel like you're grasping at straws here."

"Could be," she said. "But when we took her brother's money and promised to leave no stone unturned, that means something to me."

"Modern women," the driver shook his head and smiled. "You kittens got claws. I bet you'd make a good little WAC, you know that?"

"And you'd make a good little mute," she said. "This is my stop."

The driver's jaw stiffened. He pulled the jeep to a stop at the place where a footpath crossed the unpaved road. The path cut through the dense green jungle and twisted out of sight. The driver turned towards Paula.

"Look, you're a tough dame. I get it. But between these wild animals and all the other ways to get dead, this ain't no place for a girl to be wandering around by herself. Wait 'til tonight. I'll pick you up, and we can scare up some men to help out."

"You're a real Boy Scout, Romeo," Paula said. She hopped out and marched off down the jungle path. "Thanks for the lift."

The driver watched her disappear into the undergrowth. He shook his head, put the jeep in first gear, and continued driving up the mountain.

The walking path dipped and climbed through the uneven terrain. It was much cooler under the shade of the trees. Near a brook, a thick yellow snake slithered across the trail. Insects *chirped. Birds sang. And the humid air clung thickly amid the endless trees. It gave Paula the sensation of breathing through a damp sponge. A layer of perspiration covered her skin. She carried a round canteen by a shoulder strap, which bounced against her hip as she walked. She unscrewed the cap and drank deeply of the hot, fresh water. Through the thick canopy above, pinpricks of sunlight hung low in the west, indicating the approach of dusk.*

As she continued her climb, the trees began to thin. Soon, a pillar of smoke was visible on a hill above, and perhaps a mile away. Paula's shoes were caked with mud. The dampness that penetrated her shoes sloshed between her toes. Blisters began to rub at her heels.

Her breath was rapid and shallow with exertion. Her calves began to tighten and burn. She paused only briefly to rest against a tree before continuing the climb. The fruits of her labor began to manifest as the pillar of smoke drew nearer.

Now voices could be heard. Her exhaustion began to melt away as she approached the small village, perched upon a high plateau. She pulled herself up a sort of stairway made of stone.

The first to see her was a child. A young boy of maybe five years. His hair was jet black, and his eyes were dark wells of pure curiosity. He pointed towards Paula while turning his head and calling to someone Paula could not see. A woman emerged through the foliage. Her breasts were bare and she held an infant in her arms. She called the five-year-old child to her side and regarded Paula with a raised eyebrow and perplexed frown.

Paula extended her arms at her sides and showed her empty palms. Between panting breaths, she spoke a few words in her broken knowledge of the indigenous language. She told them she was a friend and that she wished to talk with the village elders.

The woman nodded and led Paula to a clearing.

Here, the clearing was filled with reed huts. A fire blazed beneath a spit and the aroma of roasting meat made Paula's mouth water. Men, women, and children all milled about in the clearing. All of them paused and regarded Paula with undisguised stares. The mother led Paula to the door of a large roundhouse.

"Wait," the woman told Paula, then disappeared along with her children through the woven reed door. Paula stood alone. She kept her gaze lowered and moved a rock around with her toe, yet she still could feel a score of eyes looking silently upon her.

After what seemed an interminably long time, the mother emerged from the woven door.

"Okay," she said to Paula.

Paula bowed and entered the door.

It took a moment for Paula's eyes to adjust to the dark interior. The roundhouse floor was dug a few feet down into the earth, and the room was surprisingly cool. The smell of wood smoke hung in the air like incense, but the fire pit in the room's center was an unlit pile of cold ashes.

From a small hole above the fire pit, a shaft of sunlight illuminated two men and two women sitting upon a large mat on the floor. They were stooped and wrinkled with age. They motioned towards an empty seat upon the mat before them. Paula bowed again and sat down on the mat.

She removed a small bag of hard candies from her bag and

presented them as a gift. The old woman in the center of the group, who appeared to be their leader, took the bag and murmured words over the offering. Her loose skin was thin and wrinkled, and her left eye was clouded white.

"Why do you come to us?" the old woman asked in her language.

Paula produced the black and white photo of the dead girl and handed it to her.

"Missing... dead... nearby... torn up... want to know how... why..." Paula said.

Her grasp of the language was tenuous at best, but the elders nodded their heads in understanding. They whispered quietly to one another.

The old man on the farthest side spoke first.

"We have heard of this girl's death. Much blood has been spilled upon that ground. Mostly the white men's blood now. It used to be our people's blood. But now the white man makes an easy target because he does not believe the truth. I am glad it is the white man and not us. It serves him right for the rape, murder, and evil he has done to our people."

"Wotalota! Do not speak this way," said the other old woman. She was taller than the frost-eyed woman. "This is a child! This child has done no evil to us. No child deserves this death."

"What ...death?" Paula asked.

"Lolomalo," said the frost-eyed woman. Werewolf.

Paula nodded. She was not surprised.

"Brother... wants know... how... wants... proof... how proof?" Paula asked.

A hush fell over the elders.

"Your quest is full of danger," said the old man who had not yet spoken.

"Understand," said Paula.

"Tonight the moon is full," said the woman. "In the clearing not far from here, the werewolf will come. At night in the clearing where the children were found, the werewolf will come. It is cursed ground. When the moon is full, if you wish to seek him, you will find him there."

Paula nodded.

"When... werewolf comes... what should do?" Paula asked.

"Do you truly wish to kill the werewolf?" the tall woman asked.

"Yes," said Paula.

The first man laughed.

"You think it is so easy?" he said. "You think we would not have killed the werewolf already if it could be done?"

"I... try," said Paula.

"Foolishness!" he said. "If a werewolf is hungry, he will rip you to pieces. If he is not hungry, he will bite you and you will become a werewolf."

"I... must try" said Paula.

"I do not think we should allow this," said the man.

"And if she succeeds?" said the tall woman. "Then will you be so cross? No. I say the wolf exists because the men of the village are cowards."

"The men of the village survived the slaughter of our people by being wise! Look for those who rushed ahead into the white man's bullets. Where are they now?"

"Enough!" the frost-eyed woman raised her hand for silence. "If she will do this, I give my blessing." She turned to

Paula. *"There is only one way to kill the wolf. It is a blade or an arrow dipped in the juice of the poison frog. Have you shot a bow and arrow?"*

"No," said Paula.

"Then we shall lend you a spear."

"For this cause, I will give a pygmy boar. You may lash him up and use him as bait."

"Beware," said the old woman. *"The curse of the werewolf is the curse of rage. The werewolf sees all as food or enemies. It lashes out without thought. Without remorse. It is a wild thing. It will not hesitate to kill you. Should you attack and miss, you will not get a second chance."*

"Understand," said Paula.

The frost-eyed woman nodded and signaled the others to prepare the poison.

CHAPTER 26
TOM

TOM CAME around the car and opened Lisa's door. He put her arm around his neck and helped her lift herself out of the car. She held pressure on the blood-soaked napkins pressed against her bare thigh. The ripped leg of her blue jeans hung like damp red rags. Emilio's magnified eyes widened behind his thick eyeglasses, which created a shocking effect.

"Gunshot?" said Emilio.

"Help me get her inside," said Tom.

The blue healer bared its fangs and growled.

"Pedro! Cut the shit! Go ahead inside. I'll get the dog."

Kelly held the flimsy door to the trailer open. Tom lifted Lisa into his arms. She gave a choked squeal as he did so and carried her up the shaky cinder block steps.

"Put her on the couch," said Paula.

"You're alright, Lisa," said Tom. "We're almost there. I'm gonna set you down now."

The couch was the color of dried orange rinds in the spots that weren't stained darker. One corner was missing a leg and had a weathered old phone book propping it up. As Tom set her down, Lisa sank deeply into the threadbare cushions. She groaned. Her cheeks were tight and bloodless, her jaw set.

Kelly and Paula entered the trailer.

"Emilio," said Paula. "You got any rubbing alcohol?"

"There's vodka in the freezer," Emilio called from outside. "Who are these people?"

"I'll tell you later," Paula said.

Paula grabbed the plastic bottle of screw top vodka from the freezer. The trailer rocked slightly as Emilio entered and shut the door behind him.

"Scissors?" asked Kelly.

"That table," Emilio pointed. He reached under the sink and grabbed a metal first aid kit.

Kelly worked around Lisa's arm to cut off the leg of her jeans.

"It's okay, baby," said Kelly.

Emilio washed his hands with liquid dish soap in the sink.

"How bad is it?" Emilio said.

"Flesh wound," Kelly observed. "But a deep one. You got sutures? We'll have to stitch her."

"Shit fuck!" Lisa screamed.

"Look in that drawer," Emilio nodded his head towards a nightstand.

Kelly opened in. Inside, amid loose change, rubber

bands, twist ties, and a half dozen pocket knives was a clear plastic sewing kit.

"Pull me a forearm's length of thread," he said.

"Is this clean?" Paula asked. She was holding a clear plastic Tupperware container stained pink from tomato sauce.

"Yeah," Emilio said.

Paula poured vodka into the container.

"Here," she told Kelly. "Dip it in this."

Emilio dumped the remaining dish soap out of the plastic bottle and rinsed it with water several times. When it stopped coming out sudsy, he filled it with tap water.

"Tom," said Paula. "Find her something to bite on."

Tom began opening drawers around the kitchen. He found a two-sided sponge still sealed in its plastic packaging and brought it over.

"Let's have a look at it," Emilio said. He sat down on the edge of the coffee table. Kelly gently removed Lisa's hand holding the napkins from the wound. Blood oozed out and spilled up the couch. "Oh Jesus!" said Emilio. "Move that lamp over here."

"Here, bite this." Tom put the sponge in her mouth.

"This is gonna smart," said Paula. She poured the vodka on the wound.

Lisa howled and thrashed.

"Let's get a look at it," Emilio said. He sprayed water from the dish soap bottle into the wound to clear away blood and debris.

"Christ," he said. "They hit a big vein. We're gonna have to cauterize."

Lisa wailed through the sponged between her teeth. Her face was waxen and white as a sheet.

Paula fresh napkins from a paper towel roll.

"Tom," she said. "Hold this on there. Apply pressure."

"Hold everything. I'll be right back," Emilio said.

"You're doing great," said Tom. "Just hang in there."

Emilio returned with a butane torch and a length of copper pipe. He clicked a button and a bright blue flame hissed from the tip.

"Wait wait wait WAIT!" Lisa spat out the sponge. "What about painkillers?"

"Not the way you're leaking. We just got pills, but you'll bleed dry before they kick in," Emilio said.

"Hit this." Paula handed her the vodka bottle.

With effort, Lisa propped herself up on her elbow. She grabbed the bottle by the neck and tipped it upright. The burn of the alcohol in her throat sent her into a coughing fit.

"More," said Paula. "Lots more."

Emilio held the copper pipe with a gloved hand and a rolled-up piece of bath towel. He ran the torch's blue flame along its length. It began to glow a dull red, then orange, then bright yellow in spots.

Lisa choked back swig after swig. Tears streamed from her eyes and she coughed more.

"It's ready," Emilio said.

"Wait! Oh fuck! Oh FUCK!" Lisa said.

Tom doubled over the sponge and put it back in Lisa's mouth.

"Bite this," he said. "Bite it hard."

"Hold her down," said Paula.

"Don't look, baby," said Kelly. She put a hand over Lisa's eyes.

Paula uncovered the wound.

"10..." Emilio said. "9..." He pressed the glowing copper down into Lisa's flesh with a searing hiss. The smell of burnt flesh was immediate and pungent.

Lisa shot up like cold water in a hot pan.

Tom and Paula bore down on her with their full weight.

"All done. All done, baby," said Kelly. "It's all over now, you did great. Shh. Shh. Shh. I know, baby, I know." Kelly held Lisa's head in her hand and kissed her forehead.

Tears were streaming down Lisa's face.

Tom held her hand. It squeezed hard, then went almost limp.

Emilio wrapped the leg with a vodka-soaked paper towel. Then he wrapped it with gauze, secured in place with a strip of duct tape. A quiet stillness fell over the trailer. For a moment, the only sound was Lisa's soft sobs and the four others' panting breaths slowing to its normal rhythm.

Emilio wiped the sweat from his brow onto the back of his wrist and cleaned off his glasses with the bottom of his T-shirt.

"Well," he said. "Anybody want a beer?"

The silence remained.

"Okay," said Emilio. He shuffled off to the sink to wash the blood off his hands and returned with a tall boy and a hand-rolled cigarette hanging between his goateed lips.

"Now," he addressed Paula. "You mind telling me who the hell these people in my living room are?"

"This is my partner, Kelly. The guy's Tom, a reporter on this beat. And the girl you helped save is Lisa, a witness who got caught in the crossfire of all this and who I'm sure is very grateful for your help. As am I."

"You told me about a missing girl," Emilio said. "But just how is it you ended up getting shot at?"

"We're getting close to the truth," said Paula. "And somebody doesn't like it."

"I don't like it either," said Emilio. "I agreed to help you because I'm grateful for the help you've given me in the past, but I don't like it when people come around bringing trouble into my home."

"Join the club," said Kelly.

Lisa groaned.

"Let me tell you something." Emilio lit up his cigarette. "You're in deep shit."

"I believe we've established that," said Tom.

"Not yet, smart guy," said Emilio. "It's a lot deeper than you think."

"You traced the signal from the transmitter I left you?" asked Paula.

"Yep," said Emilio. "Come take a look at this."

Paula and Tom followed Emilio from his trailer into

his ramshackle laboratory. Emilio hopped onto his stool and switched on the monitors. On the bench in front of him sat the gutted transmitter. Paula could see he'd attached thin multicolored wires to its circuit board which ran to some sort of home-brewed electronic device constructed - in part - from a toaster.

"You see this," Emilio pointed at the monitor with his cigarette. There was a green rectangle with pulsating waves emanating from it. "That's this thing you left me with. And if we zoom out here" Emilio tapped a few buttons on the keyboard. "Look at that. That's the source of the signal. You recognize that?"

The screen displayed a much larger green rectangle, which also emitted the same waves as the small device.

"That's coming from the mountain," said Tom.

"The mill on the hill," said Paula.

"Brachyura?" called Kelly from the trailer.

"Bingo," said Emilio.

Tom's face flushed. The world seemed to be spinning slowly and backwards.

"It makes so much sense," he said. "That's why there's so much muscle against us."

"And why the cops are no help. With that kinda dough, it's a cinch he's got DIPD eating out of his hand."

"There's some shady shit going on up in that place," said Emilio. "Believe me. It's like a military compound. I've had my eye on that place ever since they started building it. Maybe everyone else has been sleeping right through it, but I've got to wonder why a guy like that sets up a secret shop in a place like this. I think it's to get away from prying eyes. But why not buy a private island for that?"

"Maybe he likes having a spot for him and his employees to buy groceries?" Tom suggested.

"I don't buy it. They never released any numbers on what that place cost, but it was seven- eight figures easy. And what are they doing anyway?"

"Sending spook signals to spook transmitters you find in places people go missing or get dead," said Paula.

"Yep," said Emilio. "So, I'll ask you nicely to take this thing far off my property and keep me the hell out of this mess." He handed the transmitter to Paula.

"Sure," said Paula. She pocketed the device. "Thanks, Emilio."

He nodded and took a hit off his beer.

Tom and Paula headed the trailer.

"How's she doing?" Tom asked.

"She's passed out," said Kelly. "It was a lot of excitement and a lot of hooch. But she's breathing and has a good pulse."

"So what's the plan now?" Tom asked.

"The plan is we follow the one lead we've got," said Paula. "We know that signal is coming from Brachyura's place, and I bet my left foot that's where we find Rhonda."

"That place is a fortress!" said Kelly.

"You got any better ideas?" Paula asked. "We're in deep now. Either we run or we fight. You've seen what it's like out there. Brachyura's got a bottomless well of resources, not the least of which a department of bought cops. If you want to take your chances catching a boat off this island to go live under a fake name someplace- that's your gamble. Maybe it'll work out or maybe you'll get dusted before you make the coast. The way I see it, we either solve this thing or we're pushing up daisies. You're a big girl, babe. You make your own deci- sion. As for me, I'm finding that girl."

Kelly's eyes were hard. Then she shook her head.

"You know something," she said. "I don't know how the hell you get me so damn mad and so damn hot all at once."

"It's a gift," she said. "What about you, cowboy. You in?"

Tom looked down at Lisa. She was lying on the dirty couch now covered in her own blood. Her golden hair was matted to her head with sweat. Her complexion was wan. Her breathing was shallow and her eyelids cracked open just enough to expose a sliver of white.

"What about her?" Tom asked.

"What about it, Emilio?" said Paula. "Can she stay for a while. She's got no place else to go."

"That's alright," said Emilio. "When are you coming back for her?"

"Soon, I hope."

From outside, Pedro began barking. It was a deep, warning bark at first. Then it rose in pitch. It sounded like the wind was picking up and playing hell with the trees outside. A branch cracked. The dog let out a shrill cry that was cut short, and an awful shrieking sound pierced the air.

"What the hell is that?" Emilio said.

Tom stood nearest the window. Its yellowed blinds were drawn shut. He spread them apart with his hands and squinted through the dirty window. Outside the sky was gray. A light rain was just beginning to fall and the palm fronds danced and waved in the stiff breeze. The world was awash with motion and a dirty bug screen obscured his view. But momentarily it came into view. At roughly six feet tall and eight feet wide, a mind-bendingly enormous crab held the carcass of the dog to its mouth and dripped blood as it ate.

A scream caught in Tom's throat. Two more such creatures sidled into view on nightmare legs and unstuck the words from his throat.

"My God!" said Tom. "It's giant goddam crabs!"

Kelly and Paula leapt to the window and peered out. Their jaws dropped.

"The fuck are you talking about?" said Emilio.

"Lisa talked about this. Oh shit!" said Tom.

"Get back from the window," said Paula.

Kelly sat Lisa up from the couch.

"Come on," she said. "Wake up, Lisa. You've got to wake up now."

Paula drew her revolver from its holster.

"You've got guns, right, Emilio?" she said.

"Fuckin-A."

"Grab 'em." Then to Tom: "You too, cowboy."

Tom drew his own gun and checked the magazine.

One bullet, plus one in the chamber. He snapped it back in place. Raindrops began to tap loudly on the sheet metal roof.

Kelly had managed to drag Lisa off the couch. Her eyes were beginning to roll open, but she still hung heavy in Kelly's arms. Emilio was turning the dial on a gun safe in the back room. Another shriek drove ice picks into their eardrums as a massive claw came smashing through the acrylic window.

Lisa's eyes opened wide and she pressed into the good leg to stand, but sent her and Kelly toppling into the TV stand behind them.

Tom jumped back.

Lisa took aim and squeezed two rounds into the claw, the smell of burnt cordite filling the windswept air.

The creature screeched again and withdrew its claw.

"Christ on the cross!" said Emilio from behind. He pulled down on the safe's handle and the door swung open, revealing a pump-action shotgun, a bump-stock assault rifle, and several metal boxes of ammo. Emilio grabbed the shotgun for himself, then called out "Tom, think fast. It's loaded."

He tossed the assault rifle through the air. Tom was still holding his pistol, but managed to catch it with his free hand and the crook of his elbow. He stuffed the pistol into the waistband of his pants.

There was a terrible pounding sound on the sheet metal roof like bowling balls were falling on it from the sky. The corrugated panels began to buckle and the flimsy makeshift structure began to shake.

Lisa had steadied herself against the trailer's cutaway wall. Kelly stood beside her with a pistol in one hand and her red tasseled sword glinting in the other.

Emilio racked the shotgun as a terrible thunderclap ripped through the quaking structure, heralding a giant claw breaking through the roof. It crashed upon the table below, breaking it in half and sending dusty old radio parts, boxes of nuts and bolts, and all manner of miscellaneous junk leaping into the air.

Emilio let loose a spray of buckshot with a flash of light and a violent crash. Blue blood erupted from the mangled claw. The beast screamed and retracted its limb from the ceiling. The framing ripped loose with it and the whole back wall gave way. The storm outside was a sudden torrent, and buckets of rainwater and gray daylight came rushing in through the massive opening. The wind blew water in and the electronics began to spark and crack. An arc of electricity popped across the workbench before the monitors went black.

Two of the monstrous crabs crowded into the opening of the broken wall. They moved with frightening speed. Tom took aim and pulled the trigger but nothing happened. He fumbled to find and disengage the safety while Paula and Kelly pumped rounds into the creatures. It seemed to have no effect. Emilio let loose another spray of buckshot. It knocked the leg out from one of the creatures. He stumbled for a moment, but quickly recovered and leapt forward with renewed vigor.

Tom found the safety and switched it off as a blast from behind him sent dust and broken plastic shards flying into the back of his head. He turned to see Lisa- eyes wide with terror- lifting her pistol to another menacing pincer that had shot through the window above the couch. It had widened the window's opening with a mighty punch of its claw- the wall had given way like it was made of matchsticks.

She popped off a round, which served only to get the monster's attention. It swung its claw around the trailer towards her, upending the coffee table and dumping ashtrays and old magazines onto the floor.

Tom aimed his sights right at what might have served as the thing's face and sprayed bullets into it. The gun kicked hard and the muzzle jumped wildly upward, but a round found its mark and one of the crab's black eyes burst like a ripe grape under steel-shod boot. It wailed like a banshee and retracted its claw, causing the trailer to rock like a small boat on a violent sea.

The other two crabs were now closing in. They were nearly through the huge opening in the broken wall.

"Paula," said Emilio. "You see these little green tanks?

Paula was now standing beside him, popping off rounds at their attackers. She turned to the shelf beside her. It contained mostly camping gear, MRE rations, and a field stove. Beside the portable stove were four small propane tanks.

"Yeah, I see them," she said.

"Throw one at these bastards!" said Emilio.

Paula grabbed one of the tiny tanks. She swung back and lobbed towards the crab closest to the opening. Emilio pumped the shotgun and fired. The round missed and the sound of the tank hitting the ground outside was lost over the screeching of the approaching crab peeling the sheet metal back.

"Shit!" he said. "Again!"

Paula grabbed a second propane tank and threw it. Emilio put the bead on it and squeezed the trigger. There was an earsplitting crack and a hot wind filled the room along with a blinding flash of white. The smell of propane filled the air. When Tom's eyes adjusted, he saw one of the creatures was staggering backwards. A large chunk of its shell had broken away from its face and one arm dangled limply at its side. Its legs danced and kicked, then it fell over on its back.

"Boom!" screamed Emilio. "Scratch one motherfucker!"

"Tom, behind you!" said Kelly.

No sooner had he heard the words than a blow to his back knocked all the wind from his chest and sent him sprawling face-first onto the hard linoleum floor of the kitchenette. He lost his grip on the gun and it skidded across the floor just out of his grasp. He turned to see the enormous pincers reaching forward, opening to pinch his head from his neck. Then they snapped upwards and fell heavily and painfully upon his leg. He looked up to see the metallic flash of Kelly's sword and the stump of the crab's arm- severed at the joint- retreating from the hole in the wall.

Another explosion from the metal shack flashed through the war-torn trailer.

"Shit!" said Emilio.

"Last one!" said Paula.

Tom strained under the weight of the severed claw that pinned his leg.

"Kelly," he said, "Help me up."

Kelly dropped her sword and stooped down to help lift the claw and free Tom's leg.

Another claw bashed through a window in the kitchenette.

"MOTHER FUCK!" said Kelly. She dropped the weight of the claw and reached for her gun.

Tom groaned as the claw fell down heavily upon him, bruising his leg again.

Kelly popped off another three rounds before the gun went click.

The claw waved back and forth, widening the opening in the wall.

"TOM!" cried Lisa. She fired. A bullet whizzed by Kelly's ear.

"Whoa Whoa! Watch the fuck out!" Kelly said. She grabbed up her sword and lunged forward towards the claw. It snapped in the air as she swung the blade at it, twisting the sword out of her hand. It flipped back- wards and landed tip down in the floor inches from

Tom's leg, the red tasseled pommel springing back and forth in the air.

"Easy!" said Tom.

Kelly was on her back on the kitchenette floor beneath the claw. She grabbed the assault rifle and fired straight up into it. The shell cracked open and bucket loads of blue blood showered down over Kelly as the beast screamed.

In the other room, the crab monster had already burst in. It was taller than the ceiling and lifted the sheet metal structure off the ground as it entered.

"Throw it!" Emilio cried.

Paula was holding the last propane tank. She threw it right at the creature's face. Emilio raised his shotgun, but the gun was empty. A claw shot forward and ripped Emilio's head from his body, his scream ending in a fountain of red blood spraying up from his neck.

"AAAAARRGGGGHHHH!" Paula screamed. The propane can had fallen just beneath the crab's pointed feet. She raised her revolver and shot it. It erupted in a ball of fire. The creature shot up and fell down, as the roof came down with it. Paula was knocked off her feet. She rolled over towards Emilio's body and grabbed the shotgun from his dead hands. Then reached for the box of shells sitting in the open gun safe.

In the trailer, the claw Kelly shot had withdrawn from the wall. Kelly was coated in mucousy blue blood. She slipped in the puddle of it several times before she got to her feet.

Lisa had somehow crossed the room and was feebly

trying to help Tom to lift the severed claw that had pinned his leg.

When Kelly got to them, she helped Tom extract his foot from beneath the severed limb.

Tom tried to rub the feeling back into his leg.

Paula was on her feet now. She shoved shotgun shells into the receiver until no more would fit. She pulled the pump back and an empty shell went flying onto the floor. It landed with a hollow plastic sound.

She stepped over the severed claw and kicked open the trailer door. Out in the driveway, the last crab was dancing drunkenly away in the pouring rain. One arm was missing and the other hung slack beside it, dragging the ground as it struggled to escape. Paula charged toward it. She brought the shotgun to her shoulder and put the bead on the thing's ugly head. When she was within a few paces of the thing, she began to unload into it. Chunks of flesh and blood burst from its head. It jolted its body with the impact of each blast of buckshot, then fell to the muddy ground with a splash. Paula held the barrel to its carapace at point-blank range and fired again and again until the gun was empty and the trigger went click. Then she took the gutted transmitter from her pocket, threw it into the mud, and stomped it under her heel. When she lifted her boot, the red light had stopped blinking.

CHAPTER 27
PAULA

PAULA TURNED and walked back towards what remained of the trailer. What had been Emilio's home was now scarcely distinguishable from a heap of scrap metal. The corrugated extension had collapsed into a pile of bent metal and cracked two-by-fours. The single wide looked like a little wind or perhaps even a dirty look would knock it right over. A pair of dog legs and a tail sat in a red puddle of mud. The rest of Pedro was nowhere to be seen.

Paula mounted the cinder block stairs to the trailer's front door. When she swung it open, it fell off the hinges and slapped down on a mud puddle, splashing dirty water onto Paula's legs.

"You alright?" Kelly asked as Paula entered.

She was helping Tom to his feet.

Lisa was leaning up against a wall, her breasts rising and falling with her heavy breathing.

Tom leaned against the fridge, catching his breath.

Kelly grabbed a dirty dish towel from the stove and began to wipe off the crab's blood that coated her from head to toe.

"Emilio's dead," said Paula. "They killed him. Killed his dog. Now they're all dead." She flipped the coffee table upright and sat on it. It was hard to tell from the rain dripping down her face, but Tom thought he saw a tear roll down her cheek. "How are you three?"

"Still in one piece," said Tom. "Lisa?"

"Yeah," Lisa said. Her breathing was still coming fast and heavy. "One piece."

"How's that leg?" Kelly asked her.

"Been better," she said. "But I think I can walk."

Paula pushed her hat back and massaged her temples with her fingers.

"Well, Kelly," said Paula. "You figure we ought to tell 'em now?"

Kelly set the dish towel down and looked wide-eyed at Paula.

"What? Do you think we'll shock them?" Paula said. "Seems kind of silly after all this."

"Tell us what?" Tom asked.

"Yeah," said Kelly. "I guess we should."

"What is it?" Lisa asked.

"There's, uh... sort of a timer on things," Paula began.

"You mean about finding Rhonda alive?" Tom asked.

"There's that," said Paula. "And there's more besides. You, uh... well, you remember Kelly mentioning how there's a full moon tonight, right?"

"Yeah," said Tom. "What about it?"

"Fuck it, Paula. Let's just tell 'em already," said Kelly. "We're goddam werewolves. There, I said it."

"You're fucking with us," said Tom.

"I'm afraid not, cowboy," Paula said. She pulled down the scarf she wore around her neck and revealed a nasty purple scar between her neck to collarbone. It was clearly a bite mark; the outlines of teeth were unmistakable. "Go ahead, Kelly. Show 'em yours."

Kelly sighed and lifted her halter top up her left side. Her dark flesh had a shocking pink scar the same shape as Paula's tattooed upon her ribs.

"I don't believe this," Tom said, shaking his head.

Tom looked at Lisa. She was silent. Her breathing had slowed. If the statement had surprised her, it didn't show. Her face registered- at most- a passing curiosity at this development. Tom wondered if the alcohol or the trauma had blunted her reaction. Perhaps a combination of both.

"I can't blame you for your skepticism, cowboy," said Paula. "But ask yourself what I've got to gain by feeding you a bunch of fairy tales right now?"

Tom opened and shut his mouth. He looked around the demolished room as if it might hold some kind of answer. He spied the empty vodka bottle upon the wreckage, then returned his gaze to Paula.

"As you might imagine," she continued, "it's not something I go around shouting from the mountain top. In fact, keeping quiet is the only way Kelly and I have lived this long without being flayed alive by an angry mob with torches and pitchforks. Believe me, I'm only telling you now because right now it affects all of us."

"How?" asked Lisa.

"Because when the full moon is up, shit's going to get weird," said Kelly.

"You're saying it's not weird yet?" asked Tom.

"Look," said Paula. "When the full moon is shining, Kelly and I will be very dangerous. It's not on purpose and it's not something either of us has any control over. Normally, we lock ourselves in the apartment, throw the key in a locked safe, and let our neighbors think whatever the hell they wanna think about what all the noises are. But I don't have to tell you this isn't an ordinary situation."

"I still can't believe we're having this conversation," Tom said. He put a hand to his head. When he closed his eyes, it felt like he was on a teacup ride with a ten-year-old on a sugar high, spinning him round and round.

"Stay with me, cowboy," Paula said. "In all the years Kelly and I've been dealing with this, we've never once thought it was anything but a curse. Now for once, it seems like it might actually help us out."

"How?" asked Lisa. Her eyelids were rising and lowering like they were buoyed by ocean waves.

"You know that transmitter we found at the scene where Rhonda disappeared? The one Emilio tracked to Brachyura's place?"

"Yeah," said Lisa.

"Well, I don't know if you saw it, but each of those giant crabs had one stuck on its head. We know there are at least four of them, but I bet my lunch money there are a hell of a lot more up in that compound. If we can get in there before Kelly and I turn, she and I can fight off whatever crabs we come across while you two find Rhonda and get her out of there."

"You really think that's our best option?" Kelly asked.

"Like I said before, it's your life. You live it how you want to. As I see it the cops are no help, we've got a target on our heads, and every minute Rhonda's missing the chances of finding her alive are shrinking faster than an ice diver's package. True or false?"

"True," said Kelly.

Paula sighed.

"The other thing," she said, "is I've been living a long time. A lot longer than it looks. That's part of the package. I haven't aged a day since before Omaha Beach. And I've got no reason to think that's likely to change. The truth is when I think about time as some endless expanse, a never-ending life- it bores me to tears. Makes me want to take a long walk off a short pier. But that's how cowards talk. I never did live for just my own comfort.

"See there's a lot of people in this world doing terrible things to people who can't do anything about it. A lot of them are women. I figure I'll help as many people as I can. And if my light gets put out on the way then that's how it's meant to be. I made my peace with that a long time ago."

Tears welled up in Kelly's eyes.

"I want to give you this," she said to Tom. "Kelly, yours too."

She removed the necklace from around her neck. It had a pendant that looked like a large capsule. Paula unscrewed this. Inside was a strange-looking bullet. She put it in Tom's hand.

"It's got a special poison in it. When the moon's up and we're all fur and fangs, this is the only thing that'll put us down. I always keep it on me just in case. It's a 9mm. It'll fit my revolver or Kelly's. I'm giving it to you to use if you need to. And if you do need to use it, use it. I'm telling you that now. Alright?"

She put the bullet in Tom's open palm. Kelly gave a deep sigh before putting hers in Tom's hand too.

"Same goes for me," Kelly said.

Tom looked at the bullets for a moment. He saw his own face reflected in them, distorted as if by a funhouse mirror. He gave a solemn nod.

"Okay," he said.

"You know that's one thing I like about you, cowboy. I read up on you, y'know. Before I reached out. About what you did in LA."

Tom's eyes widened with surprise.

"I thought WITSEC was supposed to make that hard to do," said Tom.

"Don't blame those poor guys. They try. I just know where to look," Paula winked. "That was a hell of a job you did over there. Maybe it didn't turn out like you wanted. But you stuck your neck out for something a whole lot bigger than yourself. I'm proud of you, cowboy. As long as you do that, things will all work out in the end. Remember that."

There was a shrill metallic screeching, followed by a groan. The whole structure of the sheet metal extension to the trailer fell down, flattening what remained of the lab and Emilio's body beneath it.

"This place is coming down," said Lisa.

"She's right," said Paula. "Let's get out of here."

CHAPTER 28
ROB

THE PHONE RANG four times before going to voicemail. "Hi, you've reached Lisa-" it said before Rob disconnected the call. He was driving down the beachfront road heading north. Behind him was the wreckage of Lisa's boat. Now it was a smoldering heap, cordoned off with police tape. Rob had not been assigned to the case, such as it was. In fact, Chief Stark had not even mentioned the incident to him, even knowing his relationship with Lisa. Rob had to learn of the incident from a fellow desk officer bitching about the mounting paperwork of the eventful day.

"Bunch of bullshit, ain't it," he had said. The officer was an aging, black, stoop-shouldered man with a big beer gut and a propensity to procrastinate by talking to Rob. He sported a heavy push broom mustache and a hairline that receded to form an "M" shape on his head. He was pouring a cup of coffee into a novelty ceramic mug that read "this meeting could have been an email."

Rob was refilling his plastic bottle at the water cooler.

"What's that, Lenny?" Rob asked.

"This shit don't stop today," Lenny shook his head. "All that bullshit from them kids last night they got us writing up until our fingers bleed. Now this bitch's boat blows up. I'm sure I don't know what the hell's next."

"Boat blew up?" said Rob.

"Yeah. You ain't heard about that?" Lenny said.

"No."

"Oh yeah. Just happened 'bout an hour ago now. Right in the harbor. Witness said the whole thing blew up. Big ball of fire and smoke. Said the boat was damaged already, big crack right down the back of it. Probably some kind of fuel leak that caught fire. Irresponsible to dock a boat in that kind of condition right in the harbor like that if you ask me. Could've caught half the boats out there on fire. Then we'd have paperwork clear through Christmas. Be chained to our desks, eating microwave burritos and Chinese take-out until you're sick just looking at it."

"A damaged boat..." Rob stopped filling his water bottle and turned to face Lenny. "Oh my God," Rob said. "Was anybody hurt?"

"No. Looks like nobody was on board at the time. Why, you know something about it?"

"Yeah, I do actually. She came in here earlier and told me some crazy story about being attacked by some kind of giant crab or something," Rob said.

Lenny laughed and shook his head again.

"Tell you what. Today, I might even believe that too. I ain't even told you about this other bullshit. You know that oyster place on the northeast side- 'Just Shuckin' Around?'"

"I've been once or twice. What about it?"

"Well," Lenny said, "little while after the boat went pop, somebody came in there, chased two customers out the back door, and started shooting at them in the streets. Seems like overnight Dath Island turned into the wild west. I sure don't understand it."

"Shit," said Rob. "What the fuck is going on around here?"

"Like I say, it's beyond me."

"Hey, are you writing reports on both of them?"

"I'm afraid so," Lenny said. He reached over to a box of donuts on the break room table. He grabbed one with pink frosting and sprinkles shaped like stars. He dipped it in his coffee and spoke while he chewed. "I've got a stack of paper so high, if they try putting one more assignment on top it's gonna crash right down and crush the next five desks over."

"It's nuts," Rob said. "This is such a quiet place, you know? I have a hard time thinking it's not all related somehow."

"Yep," Lenny took another bite. "Probably so."

"What about the people from the oyster bar incident? Do we have any names or descriptions?" Rob asked.

Lenny smiled.

"Sound like you're tired of sharpening pencils and

itching to get out in the street," he said. "Yeah, we've got descriptions. No names yet. Guy that did the shooting was an Asian male in a fishing hat and vest with a white mustache about five two. The folks he was after were a Caucasian male, mid-thirties, brown hair, brown eyes, about five nine. And a Caucasian female, mid-twenties, dirty blond hair, green eyes, about five four."

Rob nearly staggered backwards.

"Holy shit!" he said. "That sounds like Lisa! I've gotta call her."

Rob pulled out his phone and dialed the number. It rang four times and went to voicemail. Lenny munched on his donut and watched Rob's face drop as he ended the call.

"No answer," he said.

Lenny let out a low whistle.

"Don't sound too good," he said.

"Who's investigating it?" Rob asked.

"Abshire's doing the oyster bar," Lenny said. "The boat was a fuel leak. Open and shut case. That's just paperwork now."

"What? How did they shut the book on the boat already? You said it just happened!" Rob said.

"I'm sure I don't know," Lenny said, dunking the donut again. "They just put the papers on my desk and I fill out the reports. That's all I know."

"This whole thing stinks, Lenny," Rob said. "Why is it that in five minutes flat you and I find a link between these two events, meanwhile somebody else is busy rushing around to close one of those cases before anyone else connects the dots?"

"You talking about a cover up?" Lenny looked over the rim of his novelty coffee mug and made a slurping sound as he drank.

"What's it sound like to you?" Rob asked.

"I don't know," Lenny said. "It ain't my job to know. And as I recall it ain't yours either. Besides, those two aren't being handled by the same department. I only heard about the oyster bar thing through the grapevine as they say."

"You live in the grapevines, Lenny."

"Could be," Lenny said. "But the fact remains, linking up these two cases is way outside your lane. Hell, the only person who's got both of them on his desk is the Chief. I don't know if you've seen him today, but he don't look like he's in the mood to be reading from the suggestion box."

"Where's Abshire now?" Rob asked.

"I can't say that I know," Lenny said. He looked at his wristwatch. "On a lunch break would be my educated guess."

"I'm going to go check something out," Rob said. "Cover for me, will ya?"

"I'll do no such thing," Lenny said. "But good luck to you anyway."

CHAPTER 29
ROB

AFTER THAT, Rob had ducked quietly out of the break room, peeking his head out to check for Chief Stark's corpulent presence in the hallway before leaving the police station through a side door. He kept his head on a swivel in the parking lot as he made for his car. He cranked it up and pulled out of the parking lot, heading towards the docks. When the police station was out of sight in his rear-view mirror, some of the tension in his shoulders began to relax.

His thoughts turned to Lisa and the strange tale she'd told earlier of being attacked by a giant crab. In light of what had transpired since that conversation, he felt ashamed and foolish for not listening to her. The thought of a giant crab was, of course, outlandish. But the fact remained that her boat was destroyed and it sounded like she was being chased by someone with the intent to do her harm. How all the pieces fit together, he didn't know. But right now, his gut churned the feeling she needed his help.

Lenny had made it sound pretty clear nobody was going to do a proper investigation into how this fit together until they had a dead body on their hands. That brought nightmarish images to Rob's mind. He shuddered and tried to shake them from his head like an Etch-A-Sketch.

He pulled his car to the dock. As he exited his car, the smell of burnt gasoline and charred wood stung his nose. There were three other cars parked in the gravel parking lot, and nobody on the docks.

The arm of the dock where the remnants of the Nauti Gull was moored was cordoned off with yellow crime scene tape. Rob ducked beneath the tape and walked over to the wreckage. The boards nearest the boat were blackened where tongues of fire had licked them when the conflagration occurred. It was completely unsalvageable. Half the ship's name had been burnt away and the white paint on the hull was bubbled from the heat of the blaze. The interior of the ship was exposed. The metal spring skeleton of Lisa's bed lay bare among the ashes.

Memories of nights spent there with Lisa played in Rob's mind and clashed jarringly with the scene before him.

Rob looked around the dock. On the far dock, he spied a young, shirtless man with dirty blond hair scrubbing the hull of his boat with a firm-bristle brush. He appeared to be in his mid twenties and his skin was the color of a terracotta flower pot. Rob approached this man and flashed his badge.

"Excuse me," he said. "Rob Staring, DIPD. You mind if I ask you a few questions?"

"What's up, officer? Am I in some kind of trouble or something?" the young man asked.

"No," said Rob. "Nothing like that. Just trying to get some information about it. Did you see what happened?"

"Yeah," the young man said. "I saw it. Man, the boat exploded, dude! It was the gnarliest thing I've ever seen."

"Was anybody nearby the boat when it happened?" Rob asked.

"Totally," the young man said. "There was a dude and a chick about to get on board. The dude stepped on board, then they both walked away, then the boat totally blew! It was like in the movies, dude."

"What did these two look like?"

"Oh, let me think. Well, the dude was dressed like a square. And the chick was in a wetsuit. I think she was blond."

"Was anybody else with them?"

"No, I don't think so, man."

Rob took down the time of the incident and the young man's contact info. Then he hopped back in his car and sped off towards the oyster bar. The wind was picking up, and the sky was growing overcast now. Little raindrops began to drip onto the squad car's windshield. Rob flicked on the wipers to clear them away.

Rob reached the oyster bar and parked right out front in the red tow-away zone. Up and down the wide sidewalks of downtown, people ducked under awnings and into shops to avoid the rain. Few had the foresight to bring umbrellas.

Though the parking lot beside the oyster bar had been roped off, a neon sign by the front door announced that the establishment was open for business. Bells on the glass door jingled as Rob stepped inside.

The restaurant was mostly vacant. The only occupied table seated a young couple who leaned over their chowders and whispered excitedly to each other. They both looked up when Rob entered, then resumed their conversation with less zeal.

Behind the counter, the cashier regarded Rob with a vapid expression, as one might regard a bus schedule.

"Welcome to Just Shuckin' Around, home of the bottomless oyster bucket," she said. "What can I get started for you?"

"I'm not here for food," Rob said. "Just information."

"The other cop that came by said he'd heard all he needed," she droned in a flat, bored voice. "He said he'd call us if he needed anything else."

"I'm sure that was his opinion," Rob said. "Don't you think it's strange to be open for business so quickly after a shooting happened in your parking lot out back?"

"The fat man said it was okay," she said. "He said

there wasn't any reason to slow down business on account of a couple nut job customers. Then he asked for a basket of fried oysters to go."

"The fat man? Chief Stark?" Rob asked.

Alarm bells began to ring in Rob's head. The Chief was spending a lot of time in the field lately. Stark had always been the sedentary type who kept a distance and snarled orders from behind a desk. Unless he'd taken up a new exercise regimen, Rob couldn't see any reason why he'd suddenly taken such a proactive approach to policing. Especially when this had all the earmarks of a rush job. It was far more likely, he thought, that the Chief was babysitting the investigation to make sure it didn't turn up anything he didn't want it to. But why?

Rob thanked her for the information and went back out to his car. The rain was falling more heavily now. Fat droplets plopped against the windshield and obscured the outside world, as if it were all abstracted colors and pinpoints of light refracted through a watery curtain. Between the patter of the rain and the soft rumble of the idling engine, Rob drifted into a deep reverie which alternated between concern for Lisa, a formless cloud of suspicion surrounding the meaty police chief, and the dull gnawing hunger now growing in his own belly.

A crackling voice over the police radio roused him from his musings.

"...Units be advised, 10-16 on Northside rural neighbor..." the voice said and gave the address.

Rob had had a few hunches in his career, but now the hair stood up on the back of his neck and a ball of energy seemed to rise up from inside him. Without conscious thought, the microphone was in his hand and he heard his own voice now as if it came from someone else. "This is car 1-8-7-6, I'm on it."

Rob brought the wipers to life, slapping away the rain from the windshield. He mashed down on the accelerator and passed through the intersection under a yellow light.

The call was only a few miles from his present location up in the woods. He wondered how long it would take for someone to make the connection that he was not on patrol duty and was meant to be at his desk. He realized he really didn't care. The blood in his veins was hot and his senses now were on high alert. He felt like a sniff dog with a nose full of cocaine following a trail that would lead to so much more.

The rainwater hissed beneath his tires as he sped through the winding neighborhoods that fizzled out and gave way to the palm trees and dense greenery of the outskirts of town. He had his flashers on but kept the siren off as though it would help him avoid detection from his superiors.

He turned off the paved road and turned up a gravel drive, as a puddle splashed muddy water against the driver's side window. The engine revved as the car climbed the winding gravel road. Rob rolled down the driver's side window to see the house numbers tacked on to the mailboxes along the road. The rain was coming down hard now, like a beaded curtain. It blew into the car's cab, drenching his arm and face. The houses were spaced far apart. There must have been quite a ruckus for the neighbors to report a disturbance.

The address the dispatcher had given him was hand-written upon the side of what appeared to be a black, beat-up old microwave on a wooden post. Rob turned down the drive, past an open utility gate. Visibility was limited in the driving rain. Rob could see no more and twenty or thirty feet ahead of him, and next to nothing out of the side and back windows. Ahead of him, the headlights made streaked halos in the falling drops. Something large and dark came into view. It was partially blocking the drive and at first, Rob guessed it might have been a broken-down car. Rob slowly approached and the object's features began to reveal themselves. Shock and disbelief contorted Rob's face.

He stopped the car and stepped out into the down-pour. He drew his handgun and flashlight, holding both together in a tactical stance and approached. Between the flashlight's beam and the glow of the headlights, the mangled shape before him was unmistakable. It was a crab the size of a small tank.

It didn't move. It sat in a puddle of water and blue blood. Its face, if it could be called one, looked as though it had been blasted away with dynamite. A blinking red light strobed from the top of its carapace. Rob noticed spent shotgun casings scattered in the mud in a tight pattern, as though someone had stood unloading into the creature at short range. Images of this scenario strained the limitations of Rob's logical mind. He stared open-mouthed at the carcass for a while before getting back into the car and continuing down the drive. He soon arrived at the ruins of a broken-down trailer. Two more identical carcasses peeked out from the mangled ruins of a ramshackle mobile home that appeared to have collapsed upon them. What proved to be the back half of a dog lay in muck beside the road.

Rob felt as if reality had abandoned him. As though he had stepped through the looking glass into a dream world unbound by the conventions of reality that had formed the core of his adult life.

He parked his car before the entrance to the trailer and mounted the cinder block stairs leading in. The house shifted slightly when he touched it. He decided against entering. Instead, he shone his flashlight and marveled at the complete destruction within.

From behind him, Rob could hear the purring of an engine and the crunch of gravel. A pair of headlights bounded down the road towards him. Rob came away from the door to meet the driver of the approaching vehicle. The bush guard and unlit bar of lights on its roof revealed it to be a police car. It pulled to a stop and the driver's door came open.

The car teetered on its axles as an enormous man hefted himself from the vehicle. Rob at once recognized it to be Chief Stark.

"What the actual fuck do you think you are doing?" Stark growled. His eyes were beady and mean beneath his bushy white eyebrows. His face was red and purple. Veins popped up beneath his skin.

"Have you seen this, Chief?!" Rob asked.

"You are operating outside of authority and you will stand the fuck down," Stark said.

"Chief, look at these things! It's like a-"

A fist caught his jaw. It snapped his head backwards and his teeth clacked together. He staggered back. The taste of copper filled his mouth.

"Did I stutter?" said Stark. His breath was coming hard and fast.

Rob ran the back of his hand across his lip. It was already becoming swollen and felt like rubber. When he looked up, a pistol was aimed at his face.

"Hands behind your head," he said.

"What the fuck is happening?" said Rob.

"Get on your knees and put your hands behind your head."

"This doesn't make sense," Rob said. "Why are you doing this?"

"I said," Stark pulled back the hammer until it clicked, "hands behind your ugly goddam head."

Rob did as he was told. The chief came around behind him. He shoved him hard onto his knees. Handcuffs snapped tightly around one wrist and then the other. He could feel his gun being lifted from his hip holster.

Anger was building in Rob like an electric charge. Things were happening too fast. He felt plucked from time and shuffled like a card being buried at random in a deck.

He could feel the muzzle of the Chief's gun pressing

against the back of his skull. Stark pulled out his phone and made a call.

"Yeah," Stark said. "I'm on site... uh-huh... no, I haven't yet... well, there's been a slight complication... one of my desk boys went rogue and arrived on scene before me... no... no, I've got him right here...uh, huh... are you sure?... yes... yes, I can... alright, whatever you say."

Stark disconnected the call.

"Who was that?" Rob asked.

"Shut up," said Stark. "Get in the car."

He yanked Rob to his feet.

"Don't try to be clever," Stark added.

The Chief opened the back door of his car. Rain blew in and immediately began soaking the leatherette seat. Rob turned to look back at the chief. It was as though he was looking at a stranger. His face betrayed no mercy or compassion. He held his pistol stiffly at his side, trained on the center of Rob's chest.

Rob's mind raced in search of ways to escape, but already the Chief's meaty hand was pushing him into the car and shutting the door behind him.

CHAPTER 30
BRACHYURA

BRACHYURA SMASHED his cell phone against the wall. It shattered to pieces. He ran across the room and threw open the door to where Rhonda Rhodes was trapped. Her eyes regarded him with terror as he grabbed a scalpel from the table beside her. He tore open her blouse, exposing her pale, shuddering flesh. He raised the scalpel and plunged it into her. A scream ripped from her mouth. The sharp blade cut easily through her flesh as he pulled it down from her sternum to her pubis mons, opening the cavity of her abdomen. There was a moment's pause before blood began to pour forth from the open wound. He reached in and felt the warmth of her vital organs yielding beneath his fingers, now slippery with blood.

Brachyura shook this fantasy from his mind and returned to reality. He closed his eyes, pinched the bridge of his nose, and took deep measured breaths. In through the nose, out through the mouth.

He set his phone gently down upon the desk before him. 'Don't shoot the messenger,' he thought to himself. He returned his attention to the laptop before him. The screen was open to a word document. The title read. 'The Mind Ray: Its Manifold Uses and Implementation.'

He had already combed through the document several times. Normally, the doctor would outsource such administrative work. However, due to the secrecy of the project and (admittedly) Brachyura's own personal attachment to the work, he would allow no one to touch the document which would be sent to major governments and corporations the world over and would serve as the first introduction of Mind Ray technology to the outside world.

In truth, he had scanned through the document many times. His eyes now glazed over sentences as his mind continued to drift. He thought lustfully of the captive girl who could soon be his slave. He thought of the fat police chief now plodding his way over with one of his subordinates in tow. Could that oaf not get a handle on his department?!

He thought of whom he could trust to remove the bodies of the dead crabs. He puzzled at how all three had been killed! But most troubling of all, he thought of the scuba girl who was still missing.

If Brachyura hated anything, it was loose ends.

A small speaker on his desk hissed.

"Herr Doctor," said a voice over the speaker. It was a woman's voice, the accent thickly German. "The preparations are completed."

Brachyura pressed a button next to the speaker.

"Thank you, Greta. I'll be right there," he said.

Brachyura locked the screen to his computer and pushed back his chair. He crossed the room and passed through the rough-cut stone hallway to the elevator. He placed a key in the control panel beside the stainless steel doors and waited impatiently for the elevator car to arrive. The doors opened with a swift, mechanical efficiency and he stepped inside.

He pressed a the button labeled "B3." The doors slid shut and the elevator moved upwards. The display above the doors ticked up by two floors. With the ringing of a bell, the elevator slowed to a gentle stop and the doors once again opened.

Brachyura stepped into another massive room cut into the rock of the mountain. This room spanned two stories. The walls of both stories were paneled with complex-looking machines, bespeckled with blinking lights of various colors and digital readouts flashing numbers and curious symbols. Here, too, was a catwalk allowing access to the upper level of machines. Below on the white tile floors, men and women in hard hats and white coveralls stood at terminals and walked in between the wall-mounted machines, taking readings. Dominating the center of the room, spanning both levels from floor to ceiling stood a massive tower of machine parts encased in a cylinder of thick glass. The strange device had the girth of a California Redwood. Even in its stillness, it gave an impression of unfathomable potential.

A woman in a lab coat approached Brachyura. Her heels clacked along the metal grating of the catwalk. Her hair was tightly pulled into a neat bun. She wore eyeglasses with heavy black rims, and her mouth was drawn small and tight. Everything about her appearance hinted at the restraint of some wild energy being continually wrangled into an uneasy submission with deliberate and consistent effort.

"Welcome, Herr Doctor," she said.

"Thank you, dear," Brachyura said. He laid a small, economical kiss on her dark lips.

"You have been quite absent today," she said. "This surprises me. I would have thought you would have smothered us with your involvement."

He pushed past her towards the stairs, ignoring this statement. She followed.

"Have all the preliminary tests been completed?" Brachyura asked.

"Yes, of course," she said. "We have made all the necessary preparations. We wait only for your presence to initiate the launch."

"Very good. Thank you, Greta." Brachyura said.

"But of course," she said.

Brachyura stopped behind a large console on the bottom level. Looked at from above, it would have formed the shape of an upper-case letter "C." Two workers in jumpsuits sat behind the complex controls. They rolled aside in their office chairs to make way for Brachyura. He looked with unmasked pride upon the massive cylindrical device that loomed before him. He felt a hand on his arm. It belonged to Greta.

"*Liebling*," she said. "I have not seen or spoken to you much these last months. I am proud of you and have always admired your work. Perhaps now this is done, there will be time for us again. I must confess, it has been difficult for me with you always locked away in your basement rooms. It is my hope that as you turn the switch, you may think of it as the beginning of a new chapter- one which includes me."

Brachyura wiped her hand away from his arm. He could feel his cheeks beginning to flush. He looked at the workers manning the consoles to either side of him. They looked down at the instrument panels, avoiding his glance. He restrained the urge to snap at her. He took another deep inhale of breath.

"My dear," he began, "you knew when you met me, my work has always come first."

"Oh yes," she said. "But this is not the only thing that must come from time to time."

Brachyura ignored this comment, too.

"Are the thermo-couplers engaged?" he asked one of the workers.

The man flipped a switch.

"Thermo-couplers engaged, sir," he said.

"Set sine wave modulators to Command Series One," Brachyura said.

The other turned several knobs on the control board.

"Sine wave modulators set to Command Series One, sir."

Brachyura reached under the collar of his shirt and produced a stout red key on a small chain. He had worn this key both day and night since the console's construction several months ago. He had slept in it, showered in it, and grown so accustomed to its weight that he often forgot he was even wearing it. Now, as he reverently removed it from around his neck, it was as though he was removing a part of himself.

He gripped the key tightly between his thumb and forefinger and inserted it into a bright red keyhole in the center of the panel before him.

"A lifetime's work," he said. "They said I was crazy. Well, let's see who's laughing now."

He turned the key. The floor shook as the huge mechanical parts within the cylinder began to spin. They turned slowly at first, then faster and faster as they gained momentum. Little blue arcs of electricity began to jump around wildly. The individual parts became a blur of motion and the electricity began to gather in a solid column, like a bolt of lightning twitching and dancing from the floor to the ceiling. The hairs on the doctor's head began to lift with static.

"Yes!" Brachyura cried over the fierce whirring of the engine before him. "Yes! YES!!!"

"Oh *knuddelbär!*" Greta beamed. "I'm so proud of you."

"Here," said Brachyura. "Put this on."

He pulled a hard hat from beneath the console and held it out to Greta.

"But why?" Greta asked.

"There's no time to explain. Just do it!"

Greta frowned. She looked down at the hard hat for a moment before taking it from Brachyura's hand and placing it upon her head. She was careful not to mess up her hair.

Brachyura pulled the remote controller from his breast pocket. He turned a dial on the face of the device and flipped a small rocker switch.

Greta's face went slack. Her arms fell limply at her sides and her clipboard clattered to the floor. All around him, the workers sat or stood in place. Their spines were ramrod straight, faces forward. All their eyes shared the same glazed, unfocused quality. It was as though Brachyura stood in a room of mannequins.

A devilish grin spread across his bony face. Elation swelled like a bursting bubble in his chest. He vaulted over the control panel and ran about the room, waving his hands in front of the faces of the catatonic staff.

"It's working!" he said. "My God! It's really working!"

Crabs had been one thing. They had made an easy test case. Their intellect was limited and childishly simple to control when compared to a human mind. But now that the large-scale Power Core of the Mind Ray was active, the transmitters contained in the hard hats were engaged. Brachyura broke out in peels of laughter that echoed off the stone walls and mixed with the electric sizzle of the Power Core.

Brachyura managed to rein in his laughter to a

repressed chuckle. He wiped tears from the corner of his eye with the palm of his hand. He cleared his throat, straightened up, and turned his attention to the nearest worker. This worker was a short, young man with a five o'clock shadow. He manipulated the remote control in his hand. The man raised his right hand, then lowered it. He raised his left leg, extended it, then took a robotic step forward.

"Beautiful," said Brachyura aloud. "Just beautiful. Now, how about you?"

He turned his attention to another worker. This one is lanky with green eyes. Brachyura flicked another few switches on the remote control. The lanky worker came up to the short one. He raised a fist and punched the short worker in the cheek with a loud smack. The short worker's head was moved by the impact, but his expression remained bored as if he were watching someone file a tax return.

"Atta boy," he said. Brachyura slapped the worker on the back like a proud little league coach.

Brachyura turned his attention to Greta. She stood as dull and expressionless as she had when the Mind Ray in her hard hat had first been engaged.

Brachyura approached with measured steps. He clucked his tongue.

"Greta, Greta. My dear *frau* Greta. Whatever shall I do with you?" he said. "Though I do have to say, this is already an improvement. I never could stand a woman who couldn't shut her mouth. Even if you have been a great help to me in this project, I daresay it has been a real chore at times."

Greta's face remained blank.

"You know," he said, "when you do shut your mouth- as you have at present- I must confess you are a very beautiful woman. Good eyes. Soft lips. Breasts..."

Brachyura reached out to touch her.

"In fact, let's have some fun," he said.

He returned his attention to the controller in his hands and began to input a series of commands. Greta raised a hand to her face. She caressed the hand sensuously down her cheek, tugging down her lip, exposing brilliantly white teeth. The other hand ran from her thigh up to her slender waist. She shrugged and the lab coat fell around her ankles.

She stood now in a sleeveless blouse that buttoned high up her throat. She ran her hands over the blouse, up and down her body. Brachyura pressed another button and she began to undress. He found the hard hat made this all look slightly ridiculous. All the same, he had to admit he was enjoying himself.

Brachura's grin was mirthy and mischievous as he turned and walked away. He climbed the stairs to the upper level and proceeded towards the elevator that would take him back to his private office. Below, Greta was standing stark naked except for her hard hat. The other workers were perfectly still, as if unphased. Brachyura flipped the switch to disengage the Mind Ray.

The elevator doors shut, closing Brachyura off from

the scene just as the workers began to shake their heads and return to their normal faculties. In spite of his child-ishness, or perhaps because of it, Brachyura chuckled to himself the entire way back to his desk. He resolved to watch the security footage of the incident he'd just created at his earliest possible convenience.

CHAPTER 31
PAULA: 1944

THERE WAS *a slight chill in the night air the wind carried through Paula's hair and across her cheeks. She crouched in a makeshift deer blind constructed of palm fronds and sticks lashed together with vines. In her hand, she clutched the poison-tipped spear.*

She was on the edge of a clearing. It was dark, illuminated only by the light of the full moon that hung high overhead. The sky was an inky black with stars stretching deep into the cosmos as far as the eye could see. In the center of the clearing stood a goat with a rope for a leash around its neck. The other end was secured to a heavy wooden stake that had been beaten deep into the sandy ground with a heavy stone. The goat bent occasionally to snatch up a mouthful of weeds, which it proceeded with a dull, placid regularity that reminded Paula of watching the waves crash and recede against the beach. After hours of fruitless vigilance, watching the goat endlessly chew grass made her sleepy.

She shifted her weight to get the blood flowing back in her legs that had gone pin-prickly with inactivity. She bit her lip and shook her head to stay awake. How long had it been, she wondered. She hadn't brought her wristwatch, fearing that the ticking sound of the second hand might expose her position.

Except for the chirping and buzzing of various insects hidden somewhere among the trees and the gentle slapping sound the leaves made against the gentle breeze, all was quiet.

Paula began to wonder if the werewolf might not come. She wondered if the dull goat chewing cud in the clearing might not entice the creature when in the village, fresh, warm-blooded children waited like sweet produce in a grocery store display. Then she remembered the pictures she'd seen of the dismembered girl. The photographs, even in black and white, were enough to fuel a thousand nightmares. They begged the imagination to animate the process of the mutilation and hear the blood-choked screams of a young girl being cut to ribbons. Paula shuddered and shook these dark musings from her mind.

A rustling from the woods beside her made her jump. The sound came from behind her right side. It was very near. Her heartbeat throbbed in her eardrums. She grasped the spear until her knuckles went a bloodless white. She fought to keep her breath even and silent.

As a black figure strode into the clearing from just beside her, she held a hand to her mouth to choke back a scream. Then the moonlight fell upon it. And she saw it was a wild pig.

She took her hand away from her mouth. She let the breath go slowly and this time stifled back laughter at her own foolish fear. But when she looked up again, her laughter ceased.

The pig now stood paralyzed at the edge of the clearing.

The goat continued to munch weeds; he had not seen the terrible humanoid form that slipped silently into the moonlight.

It was matted with fur. Its long snout dripped with sharp white teeth and its fingernails were long razors that shot out from its fingertips. Muscles bulged from its neck, its arms, its chest. It crept silently towards the goat. And when it came within range, it leapt high into the air and landed on the goat with a flash of teeth, plunging into the victim's neck.

The goat let out a high-pitched scream that was unnervingly human before the monster jerked back its head and ripped the goat's throat from its neck. The scream cut out suddenly and crimson blood dripped from the gore in the werewolf's mouth, its wetness glistening in the light of the moon.

The goat's feet kicked reflexively, then settled into stillness.

The wolf gnawed noisily at its meal. There was the crunch of cartilage and bone mixed with the wetness of blood and soft flesh being masticated in its jaws.

Paula's feet grew roots and her blood turned to ice. She watched as the dreaded creature ripped apart its prey no less than fifteen paces from her flimsy hutch.

Her mind reeled at the absurdity of her task to plunge the spear into the creature's heart. All alarms of reason and self-preservation screamed their blaring sirens in her head: AIR RAID! AIR RAID! She could feel the tug of her guardian angel pressing down on her shoulders to hold her safely in her hiding place.

She leaned forward and quietly exited the hutch.

The werewolf was facing away from her at a forty-five-degree angle. She knew she might still be visible in its periphery- that a sudden move or sound might betray her position. She also saw how rapidly it was devouring the meat from the bones and realized she had to act fast while it remained distracted.

Her feet were bare. She walked carefully around the back of the creature, circling in towards it. Every cell of her body stood at rapt attention. She was now ten paces away. Now Seven. Six. Five.

The rancid smell of the eviscerated animal gagged her. She fought not to gag as tears welled up in her eyes.

She could see the taut muscles of the werewolf's neck and back moving beneath its patchy fur. She was now so close, she could feel the warmth of the beast rising off its skin. Its thrashing movements almost grazed her leg. She raised the glinting spear and took a step forward to bury the tip deep in the beast's back.

A twig snapped beneath her foot.

What followed was a frenzy of adrenaline and terror.

The inhuman face that snapped back at her dripped with blood and burned with rage. It raised its claw and backhanded the side of Paula's head.

At once her ear began to ring and she tumbled sideways to the ground, dragging the blade of the spear through the muscles of its back. It wailed like a barn full of animals burning alive. Paula pulled her limbs close to her chest just in time to dodge a claw that lashed forth and struck the earth beside her. Dirt flew into her eyes. She strained to keep them open against the wincing pain. She rolled away again from another attack.

The cut she had landed had brought out a ferocity in the creature but also appeared to have limited its mobility. It fell to the ground and threw another swiping claw towards her. She turned her head as it grazed across her cheek and blood began to flow. She reached out and grabbed its wrist to prevent a second swipe, but as it pulled away, it lifted towards its waiting mouth. She screamed as its teeth pierced the skin of her neck and rammed the spear deep into the thing's chest.

Its jaws went slack as it jumped backwards. It grasped at its chest as blood flowed from a gaping hole in its heart, spurting black liquid in rhythm with its fading pulse. The fur began to recede. Its jaws began to recede. Its clawed hands became regular fingernails. She was now standing before a small, dark woman. She was a native girl, barely twenty. She was beautiful, standing nude in the moonlight, save for the gaping hole now dripping from her chest. She looked at Paula with a mixture of pain, confusion, and relief before dropping to her knees and falling softly onto the brush of the quiet clearing.

Paula pulled her hand away from her neck. Her fingers were red and wet. The wound had missed her jugular vein, but the blood came freely.

Her breath came hard in her throat. She struggled to her feet and walked over to the dead girl. She crouched beside her and rolled her onto her back. There was nothing wolf-like in her dead, peaceful face.

Paula swore. She dropped the spear to the ground and tears began to well in her eyes. She was a murderer, she thought, looking into the dead girl's face. There was no proof now of anything except that she had ended this young girl's life. She began to question her sanity- if the moments before had been a mad waking delusion twisted in stark realism by a tainted and defective mind. Then she felt rage. A hot burning rage. The urge to destroy. To rip something limb from limb. To taste hot blood from raw meat.

Panic seized her. She looked down at her arm. Thick hair began to sprout. And her fingernails began to grow. She felt dizzy. She felt her face begin to stretch and her teeth begin to slice sharply into her gums. A flame erupted in her belly and twisted itself into a gnawing hunger. She looked at the collapsed thing of flesh before her, still warm and filled with blood. She bent down and sank her sharp teeth deep into the soft flesh.

CHAPTER 32
PAULA

"PAULA! ARE YOU ALRIGHT?" Tom said.

She was sitting behind the wheel of the Stingray, the windshield wipers rhythmically slapping rain away from the windshield. The car was climbing its way up the twisting mountain road. The rain on her skin was cool in the gentle breath of the AC.

"Yeah, why?" Paula asked.

"You were swerving," said Kelly. "We've gotta be careful on these wet roads."

"Oh," said Paula. "Yeah, I'll, um... I'll slow it down."

"You're already starting to feel it aren't you?" Kelly said.

"Yeah," said Paula. "You, babe?"

"Not yet," Kelly said.

"I can drive," said Tom. "It might be safer."

"I'm okay," said Paula. "Thanks, though. We're almost there."

They were climbing the mountain from its north

side. Though the road was straighter than the southern approach where the fateful car crash had occurred early that morning, a careless turn or inattentive moment at parts could still prove fatal. Especially at their speed. When she looked down, Paula saw the speedometer read "70." She eased her foot off the accelerator and let the needle drop back to "55."

"So," said Lisa. "Do we have a plan when we get there or are we just winging it?"

Though she seemed to have sobered up a bit, her syllables still came out thick and slow.

"That's a good question," said Kelly. "Anyone ever been there before?"

The car was quiet.

"Well, don't everyone answer at once," said Paula.

"I, uh, covered a story on it one time," said Tom. "This was almost a year ago now."

"Did you visit the place?" asked Lisa.

"No," said Tom. "It was still being built. They were very secretive about it all. I don't think they ever let any reporters in. I do know that they moved a lot of rock during the construction. A lot of the construction is below ground, dug deep into the mountain."

"Why?" asked Kelly.

"I don't know," Tom shrugged. "Security I guess. I wish I'd dug deeper back then, but it was brick wall after brick wall and the truth of the matter was nobody cared enough to make it worth finding out. I can tell you that it's built up against the cliff. Maybe it's a little less fortified from the cliffside. That's just, I guess, though. I've never tried breaking in before."

"Anyone know what they do in there besides raise oversized crabs and kidnap girls?" asked Paula.

"Beats me," said Tom. "With the level of security, I'd say it's probably some kind of military contract. Weapons, maybe. That's just a guess, though."

"Just so I'm clear on this," said Kelly, "The four of us are breaking into a secret pseudo-military complex with no idea what's inside. A place owned by somebody who's been making shellfish into monsters and hiring hitmen to kill us. And we're doing it when the moon is full, so you and me," she gestured to Paula, "turn while we're inside? Am I getting all this right?"

"See how easy it sounds when you say it out loud?" said Paula.

"Yeah," said Kelly. "Piece of cake."

"Listen," Paula said, "If you want out, there's still an hour or so left before moonrise. If you want a cab ride home, I'll pay your fare."

Kelly was silent.

"That goes for everybody," said Paula.

"No," said Kelly. "You think I'm really gonna sit at home while you all get to play heroes? Fuck that."

"They blew up my boat," said Lisa. "I'm homeless 'cause of those bastards. I don't even have a place to go back to. And they're murdering people. Shot my leg. Forget it. I'm in all the way."

"What about you, cowboy?" said Paula.

Tom watched the rain fall on the trees that sped by outside his window.

"Is that even a question, Paula?" he asked.

"Yeah, it is," she said. "So what's your answer?"

Tom sighed, laughed, then put his fist in his mouth.

"Yeah," said Tom. "I'm in."

In the rearview mirror, Tom could see Paula smile.

CHAPTER 33
RHONDA

RHONDA'S EYELIDS clung to her dry eyes. It was a gummy, sticky sensation. That was the first thing she felt. Then the pain began. Her head felt as though it'd been squeezed in an olive press. Pain screamed at her from the back of her skull. One of her eyes refused to open more than a crack. The world was foggy. Her mouth was dry. From above a bright light stabbed at her eyes.

Her limbs felt like they were made of foam rubber until she moved them. Then a thousand pinpricks stabbed at them. She tried to move them slightly and found them uncooperative. She slowly pushed through the searing pain of turning her head. She saw that she was strapped down.

Panic gripped her. She tugged and kicked to free herself. The manacles would not give.

She reached back into the muddy pool of her memory for any clue that might explain her present state. It all came out of order at first. She remembered seeing a car ride. She remembered a gaunt man leaning over her with a needle. There was a car. She was laughing. Someone was beside her. Duke.

DUKE! The word had flicked a light switch in her head. She recalled racing through the mountains with Duke. Then, stopping at the overlook. Then something hideous attacked Duke. The awful image of his beautiful young body being ripped in half. Her mad dash to escape it and the ensuing crash, before everything went dark.

A tear crawled its way down her bruised and battered cheek.

Where was she now? It didn't feel like a hospital. Her room was small. It had only her bed. And why would she need to be restrained? There was also something intangible- a sense of foreboding that hung like a dark cloud in this place. She sensed something was terribly wrong.

She regarded the tools on the table beside her. There were scalpels, tweezers, forceps, and other sterile instruments whose names she did not know. Among these was something so commonplace she almost did not register it. It was a small silver key. She looked at her wrists and legs. Sure enough, they were secured by small, simple padlocks with a keyhole on the bottom.

She looked back to the table. It was perhaps two feet away. If she could only reach it somehow, she could free herself. She thrust her hip over, as far off the table as it would reach. Pain shot through her left side. And she was much too far away to reach the table with her hip. She tugged again at the straps that bound her. Her tendons strained in her hands and wrists. They did not budge. She paused to catch her breath. Though the straps were all secure, she noted the right-hand restraint was slightly looser than the left. She focused her attention on this hand alone. She pulled hard. The strap bit into her skin. Her hand began to turn purple as the circulation was halted. She could feel the hand going numb. The bones of her hand crowded and rubbed together in a way that made her sick to her stomach. Again, the tendons strained. She took a deep breath and, with all her might, she pulled again. She felt her thumb snap out of place with a sensation like a lightning bolt and her hand slid free.

The sight of the awkward angle of the thumb mixed with her general pain and drug sickness was too much to bear. She leaned over the side of the bed and vomited onto the tile floor.

Just then, she heard a sound from outside her door. It sounded like someone entering the room beyond. Her mind raced. Anyone passing by could clearly see her through the glass pane of the door with her right hand free.

There was a hiss as of an electronic door whizzing open. Then she could hear voices in an argumentative exchange.

"-- any idea what trouble it costs me to clean up after your incompetence?" said an older man's voice.

"No, sir," replied a voice in a country twang. "How-

MURDER ON DEATH ISLAND

ever, incompetence in this case would not be an apt descriptor of Greg and I's--"

"Shut yer hole, Clete," came a third voice, speaking in a deep drawl. "Doc, this man does not represent me."

Rhonda put her injured free hand above her head and rested it over top of the strap. She hoped that, at least at a cursory glance, it would appear she was still strapped to the bed. And she desperately hoped nobody would look closer than that. She feigned sleep, but cracked one eye open. She saw three men come into view through the glass door. Two of them were strangers to her. However, she recognized one of them as the old man who had injected her with a hypodermic needle during her drugged fever dream.

"Enough!" said the doctor. "I've heard all I care to hear from you, inbred hicks. I entrusted you with a simple task and you have failed."

The one called Clete opened his mouth, but the doctor held up his hand for silence.

"Fortunately for you," the doctor continued. "You've caught me in a good mood."

"Yessir?" said Greg. He sounded genuinely surprised.

"That's right," the doctor said. "Tonight is the night of one of my greatest achievements. In many ways, it could be seen as the culmination of my entire life's work."

Greg whistled a long, slow whistle.

"Is that a fact, Sir?" asked Clete.

"Oh yes." The doctor smiled with a gleam in his eye. "Do you know what that work is?"

"Uh, no," said Clete. "Matter o' fact, I don't believe we do."

"Would you like to see it?" The doctor didn't wait for a reply before adding. "Follow me. This way, gentlemen."

The three figures walked out of Rhonda's view beyond the glass door. Rhonda reached over for the key on the table. Her dislocated thumb would not grip the small flat key. She clawed at it with her middle and pointer fingers until it flipped up on the lip of the table, and she was able to grasp it between the two fingers with a pinching motion.

She put the key between her lips. Then she made a fist and grasped it between her two knuckles. The pain shooting through her useless thumb made her wince. She rolled to her side and managed to slide it into the padlock, freeing her left wrist.

"-- pure influence. Can you think of anything more worthy of pursuing?--" the doctor's voice droned as it faded farther and farther away.

Rhonda transferred the key to her left hand and undid her leg restraints, too. She was free!

She swung her feet over the edge of the bed and onto the floor. Her legs were unsteady. She fell back against the bed. It banged against the tile wall. Rhonda's heart went cold. She held her breath and listened for any sign the men had heard her.

She heard the distant whirr of another electronic door.

"-- what's that got to do with these big tanks of w--" she heard Clete's voice say before the shutting of the electronic door muffled it.

Rhonda exhaled a sigh of relief. But she knew she had to move quickly. She gently turned the latch on the glass door and peeked her head into the room where the men had just been. It was a sort of small laboratory. There was an island in the center covered in beakers and tubes. Monitors on the walls scrolled symbols and numbers in various colors. Somewhere, a machine rhythmically beeped.

Besides the door to the room where she had just come from, there were two other doors in the room: the one the men had entered from and the one they had just passed through. From behind the latter door, she heard two splashes followed by a terrible scream.

"AAAaaaaAAAaaah! Agh! Agh! Agggggggg....."

The sound made her shudder. She decided to make her way through the other door. She crawled towards it, but found it had no handle. She pushed on it. It didn't budge. It appeared to be operated by some unseen method.

She heard the electronic door behind her hiss open.

She ducked behind the island in the center of the room. She heard the approaching footsteps clicking on the tile floor. She stifled a scream. As the steps drew nearer, she crawled around the table, keeping low and keeping on the opposite side of the person walking there. She wondered in horror if this person would turn their head to the left and see that she was no longer imprisoned in her room.

Peaking around the island, she saw the back of the doctor walking towards the door she had just tried. He waved a badge next to a black box on the wall, and the door flew open. After he exited, the door slid swiftly shut.

Rhonda scanned the room. She saw a lab coat hanging from a hook on the wall. She crawled over to it and felt the pockets. Sure enough, it contained a badge clipped to a neon green lanyard. She waved the badge in front of the sensor on the wall, and the door opened for her.

She moved carefully into the next room. It appeared to be a massive office built for a single person. The walls and ceiling were rough stone. The room appeared to be carved into a mountain. There was a huge window overlooking the ocean and a single desk. The room was empty.

Ahead and to the right, she saw a hallway cut into the stone. It led to a set of elevator doors with keyholes instead of buttons. She approached this door when suddenly red lights began to flash and a shrill alarm began blaring in the hallway.

CHAPTER 34
TOM (A FEW MINUTES EARLIER)

BRACHYURA'S COMPLEX loomed just ahead. It was surrounded by two sets of chain link fences topped with coils of razor wire. Like a prison, Tom thought. A single paved road led towards the complex, with a guardhouse where a security guard stopped every car on its way into the building. A little before reaching the guardhouse, a short gravel service road cut through the woods and led to the base of a large water tower. Brachyura's company did not own the water tower and there was no security blocking that way.

Paula turned the Stingray down the service road. The rain had let up slightly, but the wind was whipping up much more fiercely.

When they reached the service road's dead end, Paula cut the engine. They were only a few yards from the edge of the cliff and not far from the fence surrounding Brachyura's complex.

"Alright," said Paula. "Looks like we're hoofing it from here on."

"How's your leg?" Tom asked Lisa.

"Pretty good for being shot," she answered.

"Can you walk?" asked Kelly.

"I think so," Lisa said.

"Tom," said Paula. "You said there might be a way in from the back side along the cliff?"

"I think it's worth checking out," said Tom.

"Okay," said Paula. "I've got some tools in my trunk. Let's grab them and see what we can do."

They opened the doors and got out. The wind slapped rain at them from every direction. Paula held her hat to her head to keep it from flying off and popped the trunk. There was a duffel bag inside. Tom opened it and spied a bolt cutter among the tools.

"This might come in handy," Tom said.

"It often does," said Paula. "Bring the whole bag just in case."

Tom zipped up the bag and slung it across his shoulder. They left the car and headed for the place where the fence met the edge of the cliff. Tom grabbed Lisa's arm as a sudden gust nearly pushed her off her feet.

The cliff was a steep drop-off. Over a hundred feet below, the ocean roiled and beat savagely upon the jagged rocks. They followed the edge to where it met the fence. There was no break in the fencing as Tom had hoped, but the foliage provided some cover from the guardhouse as they evaluated their next move.

"Look!" Kelly called over the wind.

She was pointing to a steel grate protruding from the cliff behind the building. It appeared to be an air shaft of some kind.

"Do you think we can reach it?" Paula asked.

"Not with Lisa's leg," said Tom.

"I'm thinking this is where we split up, cowboy," Paula said.

"What do you mean?" he asked.

"I mean, when the moon comes up soon, it's smarter if the two of you aren't around. Besides, someone needs to stick with Lisa. No offense."

"None taken," Lisa said.

"Why don't you two make use of those bolt cutters and find a way in up here?" Paula continued. "I'll take the rest of the tools."

"What happens if we do meet up in there?" Tom asked as he handed her the duffel bag. "What's your exit plan?"

"Keep us locked up," Paula said. "We won't be able to open most doors. If you can keep us barricaded and contained somewhere, we can wait it out until morning, and we'll be alright."

She threw the bag of tools across her shoulders.

"One more thing," Paula said. "You've still got the poison bullet, right?"

"I do," Tom said.

"Loaded?"

"Yeah," Tom said.

"Listen," Paula called over the wind. "If you need to use them, you use them. I'm telling you that right now.

You hear me?"

Tom nodded.

"I hear you," he said.

"Good," called Paula. "Let's go get this girl."

"You're always chasing tail," said Kelly with a smile.

"I'll chase yours down this mountain," said Paula. "Now let's move."

Kelly and Paula dropped carefully over the ledge. They climbed along the jagged cliff towards the air duct. Tom and Lisa watched them until they reached the grate. Kelly pried it off with a crowbar from the duffel bag and the two women slipped inside.

"They're in," said Tom. "Looks like it's just you and me now. How are you doing?"

"I'm ready," Lisa said.

Tom could sense something beneath her words.

"Hey." Tom placed a hand on her shoulder. "Really. How are you? Before we go in there, I need to know."

The corners of Lisa's mouth fell into a frown. Tears began to well in her eyes.

"You know," she said. "It really hasn't been my day."

"I know we all wanted to be tough when we were talking in the car back there. But nobody else got shot today, either. Are you sure you're up for this?"

"Thanks, Tom," she said. "It means a lot that you care. More than you know."

Tom put a hand to her face.

"I'm good to go. I'm sure."

"You know you've got a lot of guts," Tom said.

She gazed into his eyes and pressed her lips softly into his.

"Thank you," she whispered.

"You ready?"

"I'm ready," she said.

Tom led the way towards the fence. Before he began cutting, he tossed a stick at the fence to be sure it was not electrified. The stick bounced off without incident.

"Better safe than sorry," Tom said.

He began clipping away at the chain link. He had finished cutting through the outer fence when a pair of headlights stung his eyes.

"Get down," Tom called back to Lisa.

They hid behind a bush. A car had pulled up to the guardhouse. It waited there until the guard raised the mechanical arm and admitted them in. The car pulled up the drive towards the building. As it turned its profile to them, Tom could see the black and white markings of a police car. It was parked in the small lot near the front of the building. The car door opened and a heavyset man hoisted himself out of the driver's seat.

"Look," said Tom. "It's Chief Stark."

The chief opened the back door of the police car and a uniformed officer emerged. His hands were cuffed behind his back.

"That's Rob!" said Lisa. "What's he doing with him in handcuffs? And why is he taking him *here*?"

The chief led Rob towards the front door. He pressed a button on a small box beside the door. A moment later, there was a clicking sound. The door opened and the two policemen disappeared inside.

"Stark has been bought," Tom said. "Come on."

Tom quickly cut a hole through the remaining fencing. He and Lisa kept a watchful eye on the guardhouse as they ducked behind the ornamental bushes and made their way towards the entrance of the building.

"What now?" said Lisa. "Are we just going to go right in the front door?"

"When you put it that way, it sounds silly," said Tom.

"I'm serious, Tom! You know what these people can do. They kidnapped that girl, and now they've got Rob too."

"I thought you two broke up?"

"That doesn't mean I want him to get fed to a mutant crab!"

"Sorry," Tom said. "I get silly when I'm nervous. Let's check out that door over there."

They crept around the building until they reached a gray, nondescript door. It had no handle.

"How are we going to get in there?" asked Lisa.

"Watch this," said Tom. He pulled out his wallet and retrieved one of the semi-melted cards.

"When I was on my undercover assignment, I learned a few neat tricks."

He inserted the card between the door and the frame, just above the latch.

"Tom?" Lisa said.

"It's a little bit tough to get started," he said. "But once you get the corner in the latch..."

"Tom," said Lisa.

"...it should come right open."

"Don't these fire exits usually have alarms?"

As she said this, Tom's card slid between the latch and strike plate, the door swung open, and sirens began blaring.

CHAPTER 35
BRACHYURA

"HOW COULD YOU DO THAT!" Greta spat. *"Arschloch!"*

She had cornered Brachyura in the elevator. Brachyura was continuing up to ground level. The fact that she had called the elevator while he was riding in it was an unhappy accident.

"Do what, my dear Greta?" he asked innocently.

"You know!" she said. Her face was red with anger and embarrassment. "You used your technology to play with me like a cheap *schlampe!* I was so proud of you for completing your invention, but now you make me so angry."

Brachyura opened his mouth to say something, but a shrill alarm cut him off.

"What the devil?" he said.

The lights in the elevator showed that they had reached ground level. Brachyura exited and headed a short way down the hall to the nearest security desk.

The guard was a red-headed, middle-aged man with freckles covering his pale cheeks. He sat before a security monitor, its pale light reflected from his eyeglasses.

"What's going on?" Brachyura asked.

"Fire door," said the guard. "Number 2."

Brachyura came around the desk to look over the guard's shoulder.

"Give me a visual on it," he said.

The guard pressed a button, and the grainy image of a hallway appeared on screen. There was nothing but an empty hallway and a closed door.

"Turn the camera around," Brachyura said.

The guard pressed another button and the camera swung slowly. There was nothing but a small ficus tree, a water fountain, and doors to a men's and women's restroom.

"Rewind the tape," Brachyura commanded.

The guard did as he was told. The recording jumped backwards twenty frames at a time. It flipped past one showing two blurry figures and the open door.

"Stop!" said Brachyura. "Play that."

The security guard pressed play. On the screen, a man and a woman slipped through the door, under the camera, and out of view.

"What's wrong?" asked Greta.

She had not seen the screen, but had seen the doctor's face flush.

"We've had a breach," he told her. "Get back downstairs. Now."

Her eyes widened, but she did as she was told and

headed back for the elevator. The security guard spoke into a small microphone on his desk.

"Security units, code blue, sector 2. Security units, code blue, sector 2."

Brachyura could hear the boots of security personnel running across the hard tile floors.

"Someone's always got to rain on the parade," Brachyura said to himself. He drew a Beretta from a shoulder holster concealed beneath his jacket. "Get this sorted out," he told the security guard before heading back towards the elevator.

He was intercepted on the way by the ample-framed Stark with officer Rob in tow.

"What the hell are you doing?!" Brachyura barked. "You're not allowed in this sector."

"What the hell is going on?" Rob asked angrily.

"You're just walking him in the front fucking door!" the doctor asked Stark incredulously.

"The alarm started sounding. The guard waved me through," Stark said.

"Fucking morons!" Brachyura said. His face was red with anger. "Get in the elevator," he snapped. He pounded the elevator door with his fist.

The three men piled in. Brachyura inserted his key and pressed the button for his office on level B5.

CHAPTER 36
RHONDA

RHONDA SEARCHED for any clue to where she was. That she had been captured in some way was apparent. Still, she could not reconcile the terrifying images of her last memories prior to capture with her current situation. It all seemed too fantastic. And yet here she was.

It was clear to her that she was trapped underground somewhere near the coast. How deep it was, she didn't know. She wondered if the elevator was the only way back to the surface. She did not want to return to the place she had just escaped from, or to explore the direction from which she'd heard those horrible screams.

That left only the office behind her and the halls extending in a "T" shape around her, with the elevator doors at their intersection. The halls to her left and right were short, with three or four doors apiece. These doors all had small black boxes beside them and appeared to

VAUGHN VALOIS

be operated by the same sort of key card she had just acquired.

She stood in the hall deciding which direction to explore. She heard the groan of the elevator descending down its shaft. Her heart leapt into her throat. She dashed to her left towards the nearest door. She prayed the key card would work. She swiped it in front of the sensor. The red light turned green, and the latch clicked. She pushed her way inside what proved to be a small room filled with cleaning supplies. She quickly looked for a weapon of some kind, but found only spray bottles and big rolls of paper towels.

The elevator reached the floor and the doors slid open. Rhonda left the door open a crack and peered out to see who had arrived. First, she saw the doctor. Then she saw two men in police uniforms. Rhonda was elated. She was saved! She wanted to throw open the door, run to them, and throw herself into their protection. She could explain to them everything that had happened- how this man had held her captive. But a feeling prevented her. Something was off.

Then she saw the smaller officer had his hands cuffed behind his back. The fat officer appeared to be leading him against his will. She listened intently to their conversation.

"-- no thought of subtly," said another voice. It was the doctor she'd seen earlier.

"I brought him to you, didn't I? Tied up the loose end," said the fat man in uniform.

"If you'd kept control of your department like I paid

you to do, there wouldn't be a loose end to deal with," the doctor snapped.

The three were moving down the stony hall from the elevator towards the big office.

"What the hell are you doing?" the smaller cop's voice echoed.

Rhonda waited until she heard the mechanical door whiz closed behind the men as they exited the office. She knew it was only a matter of time until they discovered she was missing. Whatever she was going to do, she had to act fast.

CHAPTER 31
TOM

THE GUARD RUSHED DOWN the empty hall towards the fire that had set off the alarm. He held his pistol ready. Beyond the ficus tree, there were only two bathroom doors and the fire exit. He kicked open the women's restroom. Then a pair of heavy bolt cutters smashed into the side of his head. He crumpled like a damp blanket onto the bathroom floor.

"Take his gun," said Tom.

Lisa reached down for the handgun. She pulled out the gun she'd brought with her and now she was holding a pistol in each hand.

Tom hung the bolt cutters through his belt and pulled the assault rifle off his back.

"So much for sneaking in," Lisa said.

"Well, we're here now," said Tom. "Come on. There'll be more soon."

"So the plan is we're just blasting our way through?" Lisa asked.

"I'm open to suggestions," said Tom. "Shh. I think I hear more coming."

Tom opened the door a sliver. A bullet smashed into the door and sent splinters flying. Tom pointed the rifle through the crack in the door and sprayed bullets blindly into the hall.

"Quick, let's move," he said.

Tom led the way out the door. The wall of the hallway was painted with blood and the body of a uniformed guard lay motionless on the ground. Another guard came around the corner. Bullets flashed from his pistol. Lisa got low and her handguns jumped back in both her hands with loud reports. There was a spray of red and the guard tumbled over.

"Keep pushing in," said Tom.

They kept a low profile and moved swiftly deeper into the building. The hall ended in a T-shape. Tom looked left and Lisa looked right.

"Watch it!" said Lisa.

Tom ducked back as rounds kicked dust from the wall just beside his head. He turned his rifle and spit rounds in the direction of the attackers. The smell of burnt gunpowder was now thick in the halls. Tom saw two bodies fall face-first and form dark pools of blood.

A door across the hall was labeled as emergency stairs.

"Let's try that way," Tom pointed with his head. "I bet they're keeping her deeper in the complex."

Footsteps rang with percussive urgency from both right and left. Tom opened the door to the stairwell and

Lisa dove in. A crackle of gunfire rang from both sides. Tom loosed rounds high and wild down both directions before jumping through the double doors. He pulled them closed after him and shoved the bolt cutters through the grab bars of the doors, effectively locking them behind him.

"Go, go, go!" he told Lisa. "That won't hold forever."

The stairwell was a simple shaft lit by cold fluorescent lights. The air was cool and still smelled of freshly poured concrete. The stairs switchbacked their way down the shaft. It was raw cinder blocks for the first levels, then rough stone as they penetrated deeper into the mountain.

The doors behind them rattled as a swarm of guards battered at the door like angry hornets after someone kicked their nest. Tom could see them piling up through the thin rectangular windows set in the fake wood. Bullets popped through the doors and ricocheted with weird zipping sounds off the stairwell walls. Tom and Lisa booked it down the concrete stairs.

The door popped open on the landing below. Lisa popped off a round that pinged off the stone wall above the woman's head. She was dressed in a lab coat and covered her ears when the shot rang out. She turned to flee, but Tom grabbed her by the back of her jacket and carried her through the door.

They stood in a dimly lit room. It was darkly carpeted. The floor was covered in tall cubicles and computer monitors playing satisfying geometric screensavers. Tom pushed the woman in the lab coat against the wall.

"Where's the girl?" Tom asked through clenched teeth.

The woman had deep brown hair cut into straight bangs that fell full and heavy around her head. She wore red-framed reading glasses and appeared to be in her early twenties. Her face was as white as copy paper.

"Wha- what?" She shrank away from the guns pointed at her. "I don't know what you're talking about."

"Rhonda Rhodes. A girl just a little younger than you. Brought here against her will sometime last night," Tom said.

"I don't know. I don't know. Oh God, please don't shoot me," the girl in the lab coat said.

"I think she's telling the truth, Tom," said Lisa.

Though it felt a strange moment for it, Tom noted how sober and clear-headed Lisa now sounded. And he had to agree with her. The woman before him didn't seem like the type to withhold information with a gun to her head.

"Alright," said Tom to the woman. "I'll take your word for it. But if someone were to keep a hostage here, where would they be?"

"Wha- why would someone keep hostages here? Oh God, please don't point those guns at me anymore!"

From the stairwell, it sounded as though a battering ram were threatening to smash through the barricaded door. Tom looked quickly around the room. There was a door labeled "Nursing Room" on the wall nearby. Tom dragged the woman to this room. There was a small black key card reader on the wall by the door.

"Open it," said Tom.

The woman waved a key card in front of it, and the door beeped. Tom pushed the woman in and Lisa came after, locking the deadbolt on the door behind her. A motion sensor switched on soft overhead lighting. There was a comfortable-looking chair and a painting of a sunset on the wall. In other circumstances, the effect might have been relaxing.

"What's your name?" Lisa asked. Her soothing tone matched the room.

"Veronica," said the woman.

"Listen, Veronica," said Lisa. "We're not here to hurt you. We're just looking for a kidnapped girl we've tracked to this facility. People have been bombing us and shooting at us the whole way. They even sent giant mutant crabs after us and killed someone who was helping us out. But we finally made it here. And we just want to know where the girl is."

"Giant mutant crabs?" Veronica said. "I don't understand."

Tom looked around the nursing room.

"What exactly is it you all do here, Veronica?" he asked.

"We design and engineer cellular hardware," she said. "You know... for phones and tablets. I don't know anything about kidnapping or crabs. Honest."

Tom and Lisa exchanged confused looks.

"Cell phones..." Tom raised his eyebrow. Lisa shrugged.

"I think we need to talk to the man in charge," said Tom. "Where do we find Brachyura?"

"His office is at the bottom level- B5," Veronica said. "But it can only be accessed with a special key."

The banging from the stairwell was growing louder. There was the sound of wood splintering. Other foot-steps could be heard in the stairwell that seemed to be coming up from lower levels.

"Where can we find the key?" Lisa asked.

"Brachyura has the only one I know of. He always keeps it on him."

From the stairwell came the unmistakable sound of the double doors breaking open. Footsteps fell like rain-drops coming both up and down the stairs.

"Alright, Veronica," said Tom. "We need you to act if you want to live through this thing. Throw 'em off our trail and we'll let you walk. Deal?"

Veronica nodded vehemently.

"Good," said Tom. "Do it now." He undid the lock and opened the door to the call center floor.

Veronica stepped out of the nursing room just as the flood of guards began pouring in from the stairwell.

"They went that way," Veronica said, pointing towards the sea of cubicles.

Tom and Lisa waited until the sound of footsteps began to fade.

"Clear?" Tom asked.

"Yes," answered Veronica.

Tom and Lisa exited the room.

"Good work," Tom said. "Now, give me your badge."

The woman obeyed and placed the key card in his hand.

"When all this is over," said Tom, "there'll be a very interesting article about all this in Island Eye."

This time, Veronica looked confused, but Tom and Lisa had already disappeared into the stairwell.

CHAPTER 38
PAULA

THE AIR SHAFT'S metal buckled and popped as Paula and Kelly crawled on hands and knees down the dark metallic passageways. Kelly shone a small key chain light to illuminate the way, while Paula pulled the duffle bag behind her. The space was tight, barely large enough to crawl on hands and knees.

After a time, the passageway intersected a wider vertical shaft leading both up and down. The feeble beam of Kelly's light did not reach the bottom. This section by the drop-off was wide enough to turn around in. Paula rummaged through it and produced a long coil of thick rope.

"I figure we follow this shaft as far down as we can," said Paula. "Wherever they're keeping her, from the inside out is probably going to be easier than working from the outside in."

"Your bag of tricks really comes in handy," Kelly said.

"I try not to bring my work home," Paula said, "but you'd be surprised at the times I've had with some of this stuff."

"So this is just another day at the office?"

Paula laughed.

"I'd say being attacked by giant shellfish and infiltrating a secret underground lab still qualifies as unusual."

"What time is it?" Kelly asked.

"Give me some light," said Paula.

Paula lifted her watch into the glow of Kelly's light.

"It's coming up fast," Paula said. "Maybe five minutes till showtime. Maybe less."

"Paula, there's something I've got to say," Kelly said. She sighed deeply. "This is risky. I know you know that. And I agreed to come along with you. I don't regret that. It's just that... if we don't end up making it through this, I just want you to know that the time we've spent together has been really special to me."

"Aw, babe," Paula said. She reached out her gloved hand to Kelly's cheek.

"You know, not a lot of people could have been there for me like you have. I don't think anyone else ever could. And I mean it when I say, the years I've shared with you have been the best years of my life." A tear rolled down Kelly's cheek.

"Hey," Paula said. She shifted and brought her face close to Kelly's. "I'm crazy about you. You know that, don't you?"

She pressed her lips to Kelly's and threw her arms around her.

Kelly lay her head on Paula's shoulder.

Paula held her as sobs shook her body.

"It's okay," Paula said. "Hey, hey. It's okay."

"I... just don't... want to think about... not being with you," Kelly said.

"Kel," said Paula. She ran her hand up and down Kelly's back and rocked her gently back and forth as she wept.

"I know... it's like you told Tom," Kelly sniffed. "About fighting for something that's bigger than you. If you do that... it'll work out alright." She wiped her eyes with the back of her hands. "I know you're right. I'm... being selfish I guess."

"It's not selfish," Paula said. "It's human. It's alright to feel. It's a good thing. I want you to know I feel it too. I love you, Kel." She put a hand on Kelly's shoulder and looked deep into her eyes. They seemed deeper and truer in that moment than she'd ever known. "Right now, we've only got a couple of minutes to get down there."

"Okay," Kelly said. She sniffed again and straightened herself.

"You ready?"

"I'm ready," Kelly said. "Let's do this."

Paula secured the rope to a metal brace and threw the other end. It tumbled down the shaft.

CHAPTER 39
RHONDA

RHONDA CREPT QUIETLY across the office towards the door the men had passed through. She listened to the muffled voices coming through from the other room.

"What are you doing to me, you sick bastard?!" came a man's voice.

"Quiet! Chief, grab me the ball gag,

would you? Top drawer there. Ah, thank you."

"You'll never get away with this, you -- hmmm. HMMM! HM!"

"That's better."

"Why did you have me bring him here?" It was the Chief's voice. "Wouldn't it have been easier to plug him back at that trailer home where I found him?"

"My dear, simple Chief. Why would I waste such an opportunity as this? You see, I've got a prototype of the Mind Ray transmitter small enough to be placed under the skin here at the back of the skull. As I say, it's just a prototype now, but if this test proves successful- I'll have a member of the police department at my complete disposal, which could prove quite useful. Besides, if it fails, we can just put a bullet in his head and drop him with the other bodies where you picked him up."

"By the crab bodies? I thought you'd want to have the crab bodies removed to avoid public attention."

"Perhaps," said the doctor. "Perhaps not. As long as it doesn't get traced back to me, the crabs could prove useful as a deterrent from too many more visitors coming to the island. Keep it a private, safe place for my experiments."

"I meant to talk with you about that," said the Chief. "Things have gotten- well... let's say a bit more compli-cated since we originally agreed up my fee."

"Don't you worry, Butterball. This Mind Ray is going to make me rich as Croesus! You'll get yours, don't you worry. You just keep everyone's nose off my trail and you'll be eating your bear claws off a golden plate."

"That's just what I mean," the Chief continued. "Ever since this situation with the Rhodes girl started, there's been a whole lot of heat. It's getting pretty hard to contain."

Just then, there was an electronic beeping sound. Rhonda jumped, fearing it might be the door opening. But then she heard the doctor speaking again.

"Look there, on the monitor. Well, I'll be damned! How did they get past... Stark, these people have broken into my facility and shot my employees. Make yourself useful. Go upstairs and arrest them!"

"They're pretty heavily armed, Doc. It could get expensive for you."

"Damn your extortion!" Brachyura said. "I'll make all my technicians rush them using the Mind Ray as soon as you enter. Just get up there!"

She heard him approaching her. Rhonda's blood ran cold. She tried to run, but the door was already sliding open.

"What have we HERE!" the doctor's voice snarled behind her.

A fist grabbed her hair and jerked her painfully back. She fell sprawling on the tile.

"You need a hand with this?" asked the Chief. He was looking down on her like she was a stain on the floor.

The doctor's eyes were wild, and his long white teeth were bared in rage. "You just get your ass upstairs. I'll deal with this bitch."

The doctor's foot smashed hard into Rhonda's face.

CHAPTER 40
TOM

TOM BURST THROUGH THE DOOR, shoulder-first. He raised his assault rifle.

Lisa ran in after him with her pistols sweeping around the room.

The room was a large two-level affair with a brilliantly glowing glass column of lightning dominating the center.

"Alright, hands up, you sons of bitches!" Tom called.

Everywhere, technicians clad in white coveralls and hard hats stopped in their tracks and did as they were told.

"Where's Greta?" asked Lisa.

A woman in a tight bun and a lab coat answered.

"Ja. I am Greta. What do you want from us?"

"You've got an elevator key. Bring it here," said Tom.

"Why do you-"

"Don't talk," said Tom. "Just do it."

Greta looked around her at the scared faces of the

technicians with their hands in the air. She rolled her eyes and reached around her neck. She pulled a key on a thin chain from between her breasts.

"This key?" Greta asked, holding it dangling in the air.

"That's the one," said Tom. "Now quit stalling and bring it here."

"Are you going to shoot me if I don't?" Greta asked.

Tom fired a shot over her head. She dropped to a crouch with her hands over her ears.

"And the next one won't miss!" said Tom. "Bring it here. NOW!"

Greta rose to her feet and walked over to him.

"Take it, Lisa," Tom said.

Lisa tucked one of her handguns in the back of her waistband. She snatched the key from Greta. Just then, a sound from behind took them by surprise. It was the elevator doors opening. Inside stood the girthy form of the Chief of Police, pointing a handgun at them in his ham of a fist.

"I don't think you'll be needing that," he said. "Drop your weapons and put your hands behind your heads."

"You bastard," said Lisa.

All at once, they heard a sighing sound. Then the sound of running feet. Tom looked behind him to see all the technicians running towards him and Lisa with blank expressions on their faces.

"Shit!" said Tom as they piled on top of him and began wailing on him with their fists and feet. From the corner of his eye, he saw that Lisa was also under a pile of swinging limbs. They wrestled the assault rifle from his hands, then backed away. Stark was standing above him with his moonish face contorted into an ugly grin.

"Oh," the chief said, "I'm going to love bringing you in."

There was the clanking sound of buckling metal from above, then a large grate in the ceiling above came crashing down. Two wild-looking figures fell through the opening with a shrill howling sound. The police chief turned to look in wide-eyed terror as razor-sharp claws landed upon him and made ribbons of his face.

Greta screamed.

Tom rolled over and leapt to his feet. He kicked the stomach of the technician holding his rifle and yanked the gun free from his grasp. Behind him, the other technicians were now leaping forward to attack the wolf creatures and were getting slashed apart. Blood seemed to spray from all directions.

"LISA!" Tom called.

Lisa pushed through the roiling mass of bodies away from the manic wolf monsters. She followed Tom to hide behind the "C" shaped terminal.

"Fuck!" said Tom. "I didn't see it going like that."

"How are we going to get downstairs?" Lisa asked.

Just then, a secret panel in the wall the size of a garage door began to open.

CHAPTER 41
BRACHYURA

BRACHYURA THREW the dazed Rhodes girl back down to the ground and looked up at his monitor to see an absolute shit storm. The police chief was dead on the floor and his technicians were committing what appeared to be a mass suicide. They were launching themselves towards two horrible creatures that were cutting them down.

"Werewolves?" said Brachyura. "What the hell?!"

He opened a control panel on the wall and flipped a switch.

"Alright, you tenacious bastards!" he screamed. "Let's see you live through this!"

CHAPTER 42
TOM

THE SECRET PANEL rose seven feet into the air. First, Tom saw a cluster of mottled, pointy feet. Then claws. Then the beady, soulless eyes of a half dozen crab monsters as they poured out onto the floor of the laboratory.

"You've got to be kidding me!" Lisa screamed.

Tom rolled away as a claw came crashing down beside him, smashing machinery and sending electric sparks flying. Tom turned back and sprayed lead into the creature's face. It shrieked, but kept scuttling towards him. He leapt to his right to avoid another claw. Then a fury of fur and claws jumped over him and began slashing at the crab's mutant face. The crustacean raised its claws but could not reach the spot on its face where the werewolf was hunched, ripping away chunks of its shell with sharp white teeth.

"LISA," Tom cried over the crashing, wailing din, "LET'S GET TO THE ELEVATOR. NOW!"

Lisa ran forward and slid underneath the body of one of the crabs charging at her. A werewolf landed on its back too before it could turn to pursue her. Tom smashed his fist against the elevator's call button. It opened at once. Tom and Lisa dove in and Tom mashed the "door close" button.

A werewolf came rushing towards them as the doors closed. It managed to stick its claws through to catch the doors before they were completely shut, and they began to slide back open.

"Forgive me," Tom said and released a spray of bullets into the werewolf's face. It howled and staggered backwards clutching its face. Tom mashed the door closed button again. He could see the bullet holes close up before his very eyes and a look of rage on the creature's face. It lunged towards them again, but this time the doors shut in time. It landed with all its weight against the closed doors with a loud bang.

Lisa put the elevator key in its slot and turned it. She pressed the B5 button and the elevator slid downwards towards the bottom floor.

CHAPTER 43
TOM

THE ELEVATOR CAME to a stop and the doors opened. Tom and Lisa were looking down a hallway to an office- a solid desk before a giant window. As they exited the elevator and walked down the hall, they heard the sound of a woman's scream.

"Stay behind me," Tom told Lisa. She was now without her weapons. Tom raised his rifle.

They followed the sound to a locked door.

"Ready?" Lisa asked. Tom nodded and she waved the key card in front of the sensor. The door flew open just in time for them to see an older man dragging Rhonda down a catwalk before the door slid shut on the opposite end of the room. Amid the instruments of the room before them, they saw a gagged man, bound to a table.

"Rob!" said Lisa.

"Quick," said Tom. "He's getting away with Rhonda!"

They ran through the tiny lab, past Rob. Lisa swiped the card again and the door slid open. Tom lifted his rifle. On the catwalk, Brachyura stood above the giant tanks. He had taken Rhonda as a human shield and held a handgun to her bruised head.

"Drop it, Brachyura! Game's over," said Tom.

"I don't think so," Brachyura said. "I'm going to walk right out of here. And you're going to let me do it, or the girl gets a bullet in her brain."

"You're a sick bastard, Brachyura," said Tom.

Behind him, Lisa had unstrapped Rob from the bed.

"Sick?" Brachyura said. "No! Everyone wants power. Everyone wants control. I just perfected it."

"It may surprise you to know, some people actually do give a damn about others. Not everyone's as selfish as you," Tom continued.

"Spoken like a sore loser," Brachyura said. He was walking slowly backwards. His heel caught on the grating of the catwalk and he took a stumbling step. Rhonda took the opportunity to throw an elbow into his side. He loosened his grip and she dropped her weight, sinking down towards the floor.

Tom fired.

A blast of blood sprayed from Brachyura's shoulder. He flew back and flipped over the railing, landing in the tank of water below with a splash. In his pocket, the remote control to the Mind Ray shorted. In the water below Brachyura's feet, a giant mutant crab began stirring to life.

Rhonda ran forward towards them. She threw her arms around Tom, her eyes wet with tears.

"You bastards," Brachyura said. He ripped open his shirt, revealing a strange contraption attached grotesquely to the flesh of his chest. "If my heart stops beating, this whole mountain explodes. This volcano explodes! This island---- AAAaaaAAAaaa-GGGGGGhhhHHH!!!"

A claw began thrusting upwards about him. His arm snapped off like a doll's arm. The water turned red.

"ATTENTION ALL EMPLOYEES! SELF-DESTRUCT SEQUENCE HAS BEEN ACTIVATED. EVACUATE THE PREMISES IMMEDIATELY. THIS BUILDING WITH SELF DESTRUCT IN... 5 MINUTES."

A deep rumble shook the ground below their feet. It seemed to be coming from deep within the mountain.

"Holy shit!" said Rob. "We've got to get out of here."

"Can you run?" Tom asked Rhonda.

"Yes," she nodded. "I think I can run."

"Rob?" Tom said.

"I can run," he said.

"Then let's go!"

They ran. Dashing through the lab, through the office. Tremors shook the ground beneath them. Rubble from the rough-cut stone overhead fell in showers of dust. They reached the elevator and piled in. Tom punched the button for ground level. The elevator whirred upwards. Then a violent quake rattled the building. The lights flickered, and the elevator stopped.

"What happened?" Rhonda asked.

"I don't know, but we're stopped," said Rob.

The intercom came on again.

"THIS BUILDING WILL SELF DESTRUCT IN... 4 MINUTES 30 SECONDS. EVACUATE THE PREMISES IMMEDIATELY."

Tom looked at the lights above the door. It read B3. Then he noticed the maintenance panel.

"Hold this," Tom said. He handed Lisa his rifle and hoisted himself up on the handrails. He pushed the maintenance panel loose and shifted it over. He was looking up the shaft and could see the doors to the next level just above the elevator.

"Looks like we're right at level B3. Let me try to get these doors open," he said.

Tom climbed out onto the top of the elevator car. He began pulling the doors open. His muscles strained and blood vessels began to raise themselves in his arms and forehead, but the doors began to give way.

A ray of light from the room outside began to illuminate the dark shaft. Then a furry hand covered in long claws reached through and swiped at his face. Tom fell backwards onto the elevator's roof.

The werewolf was frothing at the mouth and slashing wildly, like a rabid dog out for blood. The doors began creaking open as the creature pressed further inside.

Tom drew his pistol with two poisoned bullets from his ankle holster. He raised the gun, took aim, and fired.

The bullet found its mark. Blood spat from the thing's forehead across the elevator shaft. The creature rolled its head dizzily. It began to change form. Its fur retracted into its skin. Its jaws receding back into its head. It changed into the form of a person. A familiar person.

Kelly staggered forward and collapsed at Tom's feet in the elevator shaft.

"Is it clear, Tom?" Rob asked.

Tom sat for a moment, unable to speak. His hands were shaking. He dropped the empty handgun. It clattered on the roof.

Another warning from the intercom announced four minutes remaining.

"CHRIST TOM!" Rob said. "Is it clear?"

Tom looked up. From outside the doors, the room was completely wrecked. The walls and broken machinery were painted in red and blue blood. The crabs' corpses and those of the staff lay strewn about the floor. Nothing moved.

"Yeah," said Tom. "Yeah, it's clear."

"Help me up," Rhonda said. "Please!"

Tom reached a hand down and lifted Rhonda up onto the surface. Rob came up next. He hoisted Lisa out of the elevator car last.

"Don't look," Tom told Lisa. He did his best to try and shield her from Kelly's body. "Just go."

Lisa saw. Her face was a shocked blank that settled quickly into an uneasy understanding.

"Come on," said Rob. "We've got to go!"

The four raced their way up the stairwell. Fire pumped through Tom's legs. Lisa began to stumble on her injured leg. Rob picked her up and carried her on his back up the final flight.

They ran through the broken double doors to the ground floor.

Rhonda nearly slipped in a pool of blood as they vaulted over the piles of corpses as they beat their way to the exit. They erupted from front doors into the cool damp moonlight. The announcements over the intercom could no longer be heard, but Tom guessed they didn't have long.

They sprinted across the parking lot, ducked through the hole in the gate, and bounded through the green undergrowth as it slapped wetly against their legs.

The Stingray was waiting under the water tower where they'd left it. Tom pulled the keys from his pocket and unlocked the car. As soon as the last person in had shut their door, Tom threw it in reverse and gunned the engine. The rear bumper crashed through a wild shrub before the wheels caught traction on the asphalt road.

The ground beneath them shook violently. Tom shifted into drive and mashed the accelerator to the floor. The seismic quake seemed to rock the earth like a dog shaking water from its fur. A cracking sound like the splitting of time itself rent through the air. There was a flash of blinding light.

Tom glanced in the rearview to see the building lifted into the air on a ball of white fire. The rear wheels of the car lifted off the ground and the front windshield cracked. A wall of smoke shot forwards like a hot breath, so thick that Tom could barely see. The heat wafting in through the air vents of the stingray was steam from boiling water. The speedometer read 75 by the time they broke through the pyroclastic cloud, 85 when they rounded the next bend on two wheels. Tom put another mile between them and the destruction before he dared to look back and saw the massive column of white smoke rising high into the night sky with the full moon shining through.

EPILOGUE

THE WHITE PAINT on Tom's new sedan gleamed in the bright sunlight as he pulled into the main office building of the Island Eye. He parked it up front and walked the short flight of stairs up to its entrance. He turned left and pushed through the glass office doors. He poured himself a cup of coffee in a ceramic mug and headed back towards Dirk Daily's office.

"Hello, Gladys," Tom said.

Gladys beamed brightly up from behind her desk. She was wearing a blouse with a bright floral pattern that complemented the perky bounce of her hair.

"Oh, hello Tom," she sang. "You here to see Dirk?"

"Yes, thanks."

She pressed a button on her desk.

"Mr. Daily. Tom Dickens is here to see you."

"Just a minute," came the reply.

"He'll be right with you," Gladys said. "How is everything? Have you been getting your rest?"

"I get enough," Tom said. He sipped his coffee. "You're looking lovely as ever."

A wide smile spread across Gladys' face.

"You know," she said, "flattery will get you everywhere. Speaking of which, I read your story. Whatever happened with that girl, Lisa?"

"What do you mean?" Tom asked.

"I mean, wasn't there some chemistry there? I read between the lines. I have a sense for these things, you know."

Tom smiled down into his coffee glass.

"I thought there was," Tom said. "But she had a boyfriend when I met her- that police officer. They were just on the rocks at the time. After everything that happened, they patched it up. I'm glad for them both."

Gladys frowned and shook her head.

"I don't know, Tom. A handsome guy like you, it's a wonder you're still single. I think the two of you would have been good together."

"Maybe," said Tom. "Maybe not."

"Well, it's her loss. You know, you look better, Tom."

"If I didn't know better, I'd think you were trying to ask me on a date," Tom said slyly.

"Oh, I doubt my husband would be too happy about that," she laughed.

"Send him in," the desk speaker buzzed.

"Oh, Mr. Daily will see you now."

"Thanks, Gladys."

Tom entered Dirk's office. He was wearing a loud Hawaiian shirt with green and brown flowers that looked incongruously festive under his manic, lively face.

"Tom," he said. He held out his hand to the chair. "Sit."

"How are you, Dirk?" Tom said.

"I tell you, Tom, this article is gold! We've been shipping out issues to the mainland. Online subscriptions are up over 400%."

"That's great news," Tom said.

"You bet," said Dirk. "I say we cover this from all angles. Get every last drop of this. Interviews, 'where were you when' pieces, the whole nine. I want your name on. I figure we can push this for the next two, three weeks. After that, we've got Fun in the Sun Parade and I want you on it. People will be looking for your byline-"

"I've got to stop you, Dirk," Tom said. "I've taken another job. I appreciate everything you've done for me."

Dirk sat forward in his chair as if he'd noticed Tom for the first time.

"Really?" he said. "What job?"

"I'm going to be a freelancer. Investigating crime and corruption across the country, working with different magazines, newspapers. It's a calling."

"Huh," said Dirk. "I don't know what to say. I hate to lose you, Tom."

"Like I said, I appreciate all you've done for me."

Tom stood up and reached out his hand. Dirk stood up and shook it from across the desk.

"Oh," said Dirk. "Mayor called earlier. Asked if you were in."

"Did you see the car?" Tom asked.

Dirk raised an eyebrow.

"Look out in the parking lot. The white Mazda."

Dirk went to the blinds and cracked them open with his fingers.

"He gave you that?" Dirk asked.

"This morning. Apparently, he appreciates what I've done for this community," Tom said. "I'm sure the fact that it was a big photo op right before the elections was purely coincidental."

Even Dirk had to smile at that.

"Well," said Dirk. "Looks like things are looking up for you."

"I believe they are, thanks" said Tom. "I guess that's all then." He turned to leave, and put his hand on the doorknob.

"One more thing," said Dirk. Tom turned to face him. "You thought about writing a book about all this someday?"

"You think I should?" Tom asked.

"Why not?" said Dirk. "Helluva story."

"Any tips if I do?"

"Biggest one- have a good title," said Dirk. "Remember, people buy the title. By the time they read it, you've already got their money."

Tom smiled.

"Thanks, Dirk. I'll remember that."

Dirk sat down and stretched in his chair as Tom shut the door with a gentle click.

Tom exited the building and made it halfway across the parking lot when he heard a whistle coming from somewhere nearby. He looked up. From behind him, he saw a familiar figure approaching.

"Paula," said Tom, genuinely surprised.

"Hey, cowboy," she said. "Nice car."

"I, um… How did you…?"

"How did I survive?" Paula shrugged. "It's part of the curse. There are only a few things that can kill me, as you know."

"Paula, I… I'm so sorry about what I did. Kelly, I mean…"

Paula winced as Tom said Kelly's name and held up a hand to stop him. She closed her eyes and turned away, taking a deep breath. When she faced Tom again, a tear was rolling down her cheek.

"Don't be. You did what you had to do. We knew the risks going into it. I knew them. And Kelly…" Paula trailed off for a moment. "…she knew, too."

Paula pulled a handkerchief from her coat pocket and dabbed her tears. Tom looked down, seeming unsure of what to do or say.

"Listen," said Paula as she composed herself, "I've done a little more digging. I can't prove it yet, but a little birdie told me Brachyura wasn't acting alone. Furthermore, he might not be the only one working on this kinda tech."

"Really?"

"Mhmm... and I'm going to get to the bottom of it," she said. "I know Kelly would do it if she were here instead of me. I figured I'd let you know, in case you wanted to lend a hand."

The sun was high in the sky. Gulls flew lazily overhead. It was hard, Tom thought, to think that all that had transpired was real. It didn't seem like it could exist on a day this bright and calm.

"Yeah," Tom said. "I'm in."

Paula smiled, her face a mix of weariness and determination.

"In that case, pack your bags and meet at my place tomorrow. We leave at dawn."

With that, she turned, crossed the parking lot, and soon was out of view.

Did you enjoy Murder on Death Island? Then please leave a review! Reviews help others find my book.

ABOUT THE AUTHOR

Vaughn Valois is an emerging author who writes thriller stories from her home in Albuquerque, taking inspiration from the energy and pacing of fiction from the golden age of pulps.

She enjoys coffee, walks with her dog, and playing music in her spare time. Prepare for a tale where nothing is as it seems.